Nicolas Kurtovitch was born in Nouméa to New Caledonian and Yugoslavian parents. He studied geography at the University of Provence and then became a teacher in New Caledonia, serving as principal of Do Kamo High School for twenty-five years. One of the leading figures in New Caledonia's literary landscape, he is the author of an extensive oeuvre of poetry, fiction, and theatre and has given readings and done residencies in many countries around the world. His writing has been awarded the Antonio Viccaro International Poetry Prize, the Prix du Salon of the Ouessant Island Book Fair, the Popaï Prize, and the Vi Nimö Prize. He is a member of the Société des Gens de Lettres de France and was the founding president of the Association of New Caledonian Writers. In 2005 he helped create the Geopoetic Center of New Caledonia and in 2004 he was made a knight of France's Order of Arts and Letters.

Also by Nicolas Kurtovitch:

Poetry

Sloboda
Vision d'insulaire
Souffle de la nuit
L'arme qui me fera vaincre
Homme montagne
Assis dans la barque
Avec le masque
Dire le vrai / To Tell the Truth (with Déwé Gorodey)
On marchera le long du mur
Poème de la solitude et de l'exil
Autour Uluru / Around Uluru
Ode aux pauvres
Haïbun de ouessant
Le piéton du dharma
Le dit du cafard Taoist
Cette poignée de main (with Annie Rosès)
Les arbres et les rochers se partagent la Montagne
Ombre que protège l'ombre
Où irons nous ces jours prochains

Fiction

Forêt, terre et tabac
Lieux
Totem
Lieux II
Seulement des mots
Good night friend
Les heures italiques
Dans le ciel splendide
Iamelé and Willidone

Theatre

Le sentier Kaawenya
Les dieux sont borgnes (with Pierre Gope)
La commande
La Balançoire

Nicolas Kurtovitch

By the Edge of the Sea

SHORT STORIES

Translated from the French by Anthony Nanson

AWEN

Stroud

First published as *Forêt, terre et tabac* in 1992 by Les éditions du Niaouli
Second edition 1997

This English edition first published in 2018 by Awen Publications
12 Belle Vue Close, Stroud, GL5 1ND, England
www.awenpublications.co.uk

Copyright © 1992, 1997, 2018 Nicolas Kurtovitch
English translation and introduction © 2018 Anthony Nanson

Nicolas Kurtovitch has asserted his right in accordance with the Copyright, Designs and Patents Act 1988 to be identified as the author of this book

Cover design: Kirsty Hartsiotis
Cover photo: Anthony Nanson
Editing: Richard Selby

ISBN 978-1-906900-53-3

À ma Nicole

Contents

Introduction by Anthony Nanson	1
Earth, Trees, and Tobacco	7
Vigil	16
Market Women	29
By the Edge of the Sea – I	34
By the Edge of the Sea – II	47
By the Edge of the Sea – III	51
One Tree	55
Inside	60
Alma	71
Desert Dreaming	79
Brisbane on the Beach	86
Sydney by the Sea	94

Introduction

I first met Nicolas Kurtovitch at a gathering of the Association of New Caledonian Writers at Koné, the administrative centre of the Northern Province of New Caledonia. I had previously read a number of his books and had especially enjoyed *Forêt, terre et tabac*, his first collection of short stories.[1] I loved the stories in part because of a nexus of themes that are close to my own heart: the enchantment of place in the evocation of physical settings; an enchantment too of the conscious moment; a big-hearted engagement with indigenous cultures and perspectives, especially those of the Kanak of Nicolas' native land; and arising from all these a sense of metaphysical possibility permeating beyond what the eye can see. But I loved also his style. His French prose is beguilingly simple yet animated by the rhythms and energy of poetry. It is a delight to read, whatever is happening in the story, whether that be touching or melancholy. So much so that, a year before I met Nicolas, I was moved on a whim to begin translating one of the stories in *Forêt, terre et tabac* into English.

New Caledonia, where Nicolas was born and lives, is a French-speaking country in the South Pacific, a place so little known in Britain that maps of the region in books about exploration or anthropology sometimes show all the surrounding countries – Australia, Papua New Guinea, the Solomon Islands, Vanuatu, New Zealand – but only a gap where New Caledonia should be. The main island of the archipelago – Grande Terre – is in fact one of the largest islands in the Pacific. The guidebooks usually describe it as 'cigar shaped'. Its mountains rise to 1600 metres and it is encircled by an enormous lagoon – the biggest in the world – and a number of smaller coral islands.

One of New Caledonia's distinctions is its amazing biodiversity, especially of plant species, three-quarters of which are found nowhere else; a level of endemism matched only by Madagascar. Another is its demographic make-up: besides the indigenous Kanak, there is a large population of European settlers, dating back to the country's annexation by France in the nineteenth century, as well as other substantial immigrant communities, mainly Polynesian, Indonesian, and Vietnamese. Needless to say, the colonial experience has led to conflict, but such demographic diversity is also a source of tremendous cultural richness and possibility. The Kanak comprise twenty-eight different language groups, none of which is dominant, making it inevitable that French should serve as the lingua franca for all the ethnic groups. In recent decades a vibrant literary scene has flourished in New Caledonia, involving Kanak, Europeans, and others, all writing in French. In this literary flowering Nicolas Kurtovitch has been a major figure. He has been prolific in all the principal genres – poetry, fiction, theatre, essays – and he has pulled his weight to support other writers in his country, serving as the founding president of the Association of New Caledonian Writers from 1996 to 2006.

Whereas Nicolas' father was a Yugoslav immigrant from Sarajevo, his mother was descended from a Caledonian settler family whose line goes all the way back to a Marist brother who arrived in the archipelago as a missionary in 1843. Nicolas is keenly aware of the injustices visited upon the indigenous people by French colonialism and of the discontent that continues to this day. He recognises that the land has a sacred bond to the

Introduction

Kanak, but at the same time he honours it as having given breath to his own life. In his career as a teacher, he has helped to improve the life chances of generations of young Kanak, first on the island of Lifou and then in his twenty-five years as principal of Do Kamo High School in Nouméa. In his writing – as the leading anglophone scholar of New Caledonian literature, Raylene Ramsay, has elucidated[2] – Nicolas has sought to transcend presumptions of polarised opposition between the indigenous and immigrant communities by presenting the living complexity of 'interfaces' between cultures, honouring the differences between them but also seeking the possibility of exchange and dialogue that could help new ways of living together to emerge. This spirit of dialogue is demonstrated in two published collaborations with Kanak writers: the play *Les dieux sont borgnes* (2002), which Nicolas co-wrote with Pierre Gope, and a collection of poems, *Dire le vrai* (1999), co-written with the pre-eminent Kanak literary figure, Déwé Gorodey, New Caledonia's long-serving minister of culture. At the same time, his writing evinces an openness to the world. Nicolas has travelled extensively, and his thinking and writing have been influenced not only by European and Kanak cultures but also by his engagement with, for example, Australian Aboriginal perspectives and Chinese and Japanese poetry and spirituality.

When we come, then, to the stories in *Forêt, terre et tabac* – published here as *By the Edge of the Sea* – we encounter fluid and varied handling of matters of identity. Some of the stories are clearly set in New Caledonia. Others are clearly set elsewhere – in Australia for example. In yet others the setting is undefined, even to the extent of whether it's in the northern or the southern hemisphere. There are characters in some stories who are clearly Kanak, and some involve encounters between Kanak and non-Kanak. There are characters who are evidently Aboriginal, or mixed race, or European. But in other stories the ethnicity of the characters is uncertain; this very uncertainty allows the story's particular focus to affirm a universality of human experience.

An article in the four-volume *Chroniques du pays kanak* explains how in the story 'Veillée' (here titled 'Vigil') Nicolas reworks material from localised Kanak folktales in such a way as to universalise its reception by a wider audience.[3] The affirmative tone of this article – in the context of an encyclopaedia celebratory of Kanak culture and following a series of articles problematising the efforts of previous European interpreters of Kanak oral tradition – strikes me as a measure of his success in negotiating the moral minefield of literary engagement with another culture. His overtly literary style of narration signals that he does not claim authoritative authenticity in his representation of the other; he presents, rather, his own experiential and imaginative responses to it. 'Vigil' conflates into a single narrative several Kanak tales from those collected by the ethnographer Maurice Leenhardt[4] and in doing so, observes Ramsay, forges a synthesis of the voices of oral storytelling and modernist stream of consciousness. In translating this story I found it useful to refer to Leenhardt's transcripts, and indeed his footnote comments, in order to comprehend certain nuances of the cultural context.

Which brings me to the question of how, or whether, to translate terms referring to local cultural phenomena in those stories which have a Kanak setting. Owing to the absence of an indigenous lingua franca, French expressions are routinely used in New Caledonia for such things as the central avenue through a Kanak settlement ('allée centrale') and the traditional thatched Kanak house ('case' or 'grande case'); these French terms are sometimes preserved in English editions of anthropological works. I decided that it would be truer to the fluency of Nicolas' style to put these into English equivalents. However, one term was problematic: 'champs'. It's the usual French word for

Introduction

'field', but the mental image conjured by 'field' does not match at all the cluttered, cosy appearance of the ubiquitous Kanak vegetable plots that are referred to as 'champs' in Nicolas' stories. Neither 'smallholding' nor 'garden' nor 'allotment' nor 'farm' has quite the right connotation either. With Nicolas' assent I resorted to the Swahili word 'shamba', not to suggest there is any cultural connection between East Africa and New Caledonia, but on grounds that the term has been adopted in English to refer to (East African) subsistence farms which do have a superficial similarity to the Kanak cultivated plots. Moreover, the sound of the word 'shamba' happens to be close to that of French 'champs'.

That Nicolas writes with such a mastery of rhythm makes another kind of demand on the translator, and I am heartened by his generous compliments on that score. He also uses tenses in complex ways. In the case of 'Vigil' this has partly to do with the Kanak convention of using the present tense in storytelling, but Nicolas' shifts of tense also reflect the weaving of consciousness back and forth through time and thus required very careful consideration. Finally, deliberate ambiguity is one of his work's literary hallmarks; often a story will turn upon particular nuances of interpretation which he leaves it to the reader to contemplate. I use the word 'contemplate' advisedly, for there is something of the Zen koan in Nicolas' stories, a structure of enquiry that opens up in the mind a space beyond words.

I am most grateful to Nicolas for trusting me to translate this book and make it available to the English-speaking world. I am thankful also to the many individuals in New Caledonia who aided my travels there with tremendous kindness and hospitality – especially to my generous hosts in Nouméa, Patrice Fesselier-Soerip and François Tran-Hong, and on Lifou, Béatrice Camallonga, and to Waej Juni-Génin and Claudine Jacques, who arranged for me to attend the meeting in Koné.

By the Edge of the Sea

My thanks also to Kirsty Hartsiotis, Laura Kinnear, Chantelle Smith, Alistair McNaught, and Richard Selby for their comments on the English text. I hope this publication will be a step towards making Nicolas' work more widely known outside the Francophonie, as it deserves to be, and indeed to placing New Caledonia more firmly on the map. Progressive elements in that country seek for it a greater visibility in the world, and, in return, I believe, the people of New Caledonia – the ecologically sensitive weltanschauung of the Kanak tribes and the brave pursuit of a common destiny in a land containing such contrasting cultures – have something to teach the world. To such dynamics of exchange Nicolas Kurtovitch's work makes a heartfelt and gracious contribution.

Anthony Nanson

[1] Nicolas Kurtovitch, *Forêt, terre et tabac*, Niaouli, Noumêa, 1992.
[2] Raylene Ramsay (ed.), *Nights of Storytelling: A Cultural History of Kanaky–New Caledonia*, University of Hawai'i Press, Honolulu, 2011; idem, *The Literatures of the French Pacific: Reconfiguring Hybridity*, Liverpool University Press, Liverpool, 2014.
[3] Orso Filippi & Frédéric Angleviel (eds), *Chroniques du pays kanak. Tome 3, Arts et lettres*, Planète Mémo, Nouméa, 2000.
[4] Maurice Leenhardt, *Documents néo-calédoniens*, Institut d'Ethnologie, Paris, 1932.

Earth, Trees, and Tobacco

Every day after work, whether he finished at 4.30 or 6.30, Jacques took up his machete, his woven bag in which he carried his tobacco, the things to light a fire, a few packets of seeds, and some other little secrets ... He would say nothing to anyone, never asked anyone to come with him. He would cross the sports field, pass in front of the headmaster's house, walk a couple of hundred metres on the tarmac road, and then turn left on to a little path and disappear into the forest.

Once in the forest, he would walk for another three-quarters of an hour to an hour till he reached his plot of land. *His land!* The land, of course, didn't actually belong to him; the landowners had given him the right to use this plot as seemed best to him. Jacques had thought to make a smallholding there, not a very big one, but a nice shamba all the same, which was sure to be productive. After eighteen days now of working there regularly, it had begun to take shape. The perfectly cleared space could be planted or sown. Its perimeter was defined by the forest itself. There were still a few large stones in places, but nothing could be done about them; these stones were like icebergs and to dislodge them would have required the use of a crane, ruining the ambience of the place. Anyone would have been proud of the work he'd done. The smoke rising from the two fireplaces where he was burning the branches, trunks, and uprooted stumps gave the clearing another dimension. You could sense he hadn't laboured here purely out of a taste for hard work or to improve the fare that would be appearing on his table. No, his frequent trips into the forest had served just as much to take him on a journey into himself, seeking nothing in particular – except to feel alive.

But Jacques was not satisfied. He was sitting on one of the rocks and observing the land, the half-charred trunks that remained, the mounds of earth he'd begun to shape, and telling himself that nothing was going right, that he needed to start all over again. He really wasn't happy; he couldn't bring himself to start sowing the maize and vegetables, or making the holes in which to plant the sprouting tubers. He said to himself that he'd come back another time, perhaps tomorrow, and do it all again, clear some new ground to make a shamba acceptable at least as one made by a child from the village, since he was obviously incapable of making one fitting for an adult. Before he went on his way – dusk was already falling – he swept his gaze slowly across the whole place, noting here a tree with a north-pointing branch sharply bent like an elbow, there one of those rocks that couldn't be removed, on which he had the habit of leaning the handle of his rake, and over there, by the entrance of this little man-made clearing – if you came by the usual way – the remains of the first fire he'd made, now two weeks ago.

Nobody saw him at work the next day. It was Friday and, as he had a class only the first hour of the morning, no one was unduly worried. The headmaster looked for him in a couple of different places and, failing to find him, presumed he must have spent the night at a friend's house and not woken up in time. They saw nothing of him in the afternoon either, when he had two hours of lessons with two different classes; they sent the pupils to the sports field and concluded that Jacques must have been very tired.

In fact he'd got up very early, about four o'clock. He'd taken

Earth, Trees, and Tobacco

his usual bag, slipped into it the usual things, then, machete in hand, he'd left the station, crossed the tarmac road, turned left on to the path that would take him to his shamba. Upon arriving, he gave the previous days' work only a quick glance before he crossed the cleared ground, hung his bag on a severed branch, lifted his machete, and with one blow sliced off the first branch in reach. With this action he began a new trajectory through the bush. Tirelessly he raised then swung down the knife, cutting, trimming, tearing away branches, shrubs, and shallow roots. He left the big trees and the deeper roots for later. Without thinking about it, he instinctively found a particular rhythm of work: an hour of cutting preceded an hour of working with his bare hands to pull up the stumps and pile in heaps the branches and foliage that had fallen on the ground. After two cycles of this, he stopped, put down the machete and his hook made from a cleverly bent fork, smoked a cigarette or two, and then, taking up the axe he always left in the shamba, he made a start on the big trees that he'd known would have to be removed if and when he encountered them. He left a few of them, generally the more leafy ones, or those which had grown the straightest and tallest. He left them out of respect or simply out of admiration of their beauty – for the sake of a bunch of leaves reaching to the sky, or a magnificent trunk, strong and rough, whose grip you could imagine deep into the earth. He might leave too a stump broader than the others, or a rock that barely pierced above the soil. Some trees he left because he didn't have the technical know-how to fell them properly and he feared he might ineptly leave traces that would look uncouth to the eyes of a well-informed passer-by. After hours of unremitting toil, Jacques would turn round to inspect his work, hoping each time to see the shamba, bared anew, that he'd been trying to clear since the morning. Each time, his hopes were thwarted and he didn't like what he saw, always finding fault with something, be it an area too poorly cleared, or another too denuded, or that the whole look of the place lacked balance because he'd cut too far in one direction and the geometrical configuration bounded by the remaining trees and bushes didn't please him at all, awaking in him no word, no feeling, no emotion. Each time that he resumed work, he hoped the sum of what he'd done would breathe him a word of peace, telling him that he could at last stop, be content, that the land, once planted, would be beautiful and bounteous. But nothing like that happened.

Disappointed, Jacques took up his knife, moved his bag and axe, and launched into another session of hacking, of gathering, hoping that sheer instinct alone would guide his arm and his steps in the best direction.

Late in the afternoon – the sun was about to disappear behind the cliff along the edge of the sea – he met someone. The person was sitting under the shelter of a big tree; an old man, smoking as he watched Jacques tackle a clump of lantanas. When Jacques spotted him he was not completely surprised; it was as if since the start of the day he'd been expecting to meet him. He had the strange feeling that since he'd come back to his shamba he'd been working in the presence of this old man. He remembered conversing with him in his thoughts, asking him questions about how to cut this branch, or that tree, or asking him if he should continue in this direction. Sometimes he had fallen silent, hoping for a word from the old man, a word that would have let him feel a bit surer about his work. Jacques was not entirely certain whether he had really spoken with this man or whether it was just that seeing him now had made him imagine he'd already met him.

Jacques put down his machete, picked up his bag, and joined the old man in the shade of the tree. He rolled a cigarette and offered the man one. He said nothing, waiting for the man to speak first. A space of silence. Jacques could hear the forest creatures moving in the undergrowth and on the lower branches.

The old man said, 'I'm going to talk to you about the old ones of your family; I'm going to talk to you about your ancestors. You'll achieve nothing unless you think of them continually while clearing your bit of land. You'll achieve nothing unless you think of them when you're seeking which direction you should continue your work. You'll achieve nothing unless you think of them when you're tired and want to give up. The old ones know everything; they know everything and they know how to instruct you. They have a language that's stronger than death, or time, or distance. They have a language that maybe nobody would know how to write, but yet, despite that, or perhaps because of that, endures through time. If you learn this language, if you're receptive, if you open your heart to what's around you, if you open your heart to the nature around you, then you too will know everything; you'll know where you need to go, you'll know how you should go there, you'll know where to strike the axe and where not to, you'll sense the moment when you should take a new direction so that your shamba may be the true reflection of what you desire and what you see. Your shamba will reflect who you are; it will be your inner being that is hidden in everyday life and longs only to be revealed. It will have the colour of your heart; it will have the smell of your skin and the strength of your courage and your love. It will reveal your deep thoughts, those which make you stand up straight on the earth, your head tirelessly supporting the weight of the sky; those which make you human rather than animal. And when you have misgivings you have only to come here to collect your thoughts and to listen. To listen to the voice of your ancestors who will dwell here, for you'll have made them this dwelling place, you'll have prepared for them this piece of land, they'll have accompanied your every action here.'

In the long silence that ensued, Jacques thought of nothing. He didn't try to make sense of the words he'd heard. He did not dwell on them. The two men were sitting side by side. Just sitting there. Simply, quietly, sitting.

The old man then spoke a few more words: 'It's good to want to clear the bush, it's good to want to plant things, it's good also to have contact with nature through toil and sweat – but all of that is useless if it doesn't produce some kilos of yams as well, and worse yet if you don't listen to the old ones and don't learn their language. Be humble and modest and your actions will become easier; be humble and modest and you will go the distance. Do not think too much about the plans in your head. Listen to the voices in your belly. Maybe this is the one word to say to you: *Listen*.'

At last he was silent.

Jacques stood up, walked to the branch where he'd hung his bag, and took out some tobacco. When he turned round, the old man was gone. He wondered if he'd been dreaming, if he'd been hallucinating because he was so tired. But it didn't really matter; the main thing was that he'd heard something profound and it had touched him. Perhaps his tiredness had allowed a voice to wake that had long been dormant … That was surely a good thing.

He threw himself back to work. It was night, he shouldn't have been able to see much, and yet he could see well enough to do what he had to do. Hacking, trimming, hauling the branches, uprooting, gathering the wood and foliage, making small fires, grubbing up stumps, dealing violent axe blows – you might have thought he was a maniac – upon the thicker branches and trunks. Cutting again, heedless of the grazing and tearing of the skin on his fingers and his palms, the ripping of his shirt that he hadn't taken off. He knew what he had to do and he was doing it, less frenetically now, patiently even. He would take a moment to turn round and look behind him. He certainly never saw the place where he'd started; in fact he no longer knew where he was. So what? He had to trust ... At daybreak, exhausted, his muscles so weak that he could no longer grip his machete or his hook, slumping down on the ground, he took a good long look at his night's work. He thought he was happy, he thought he was satisfied ... Alas, soon enough he couldn't bear to look any longer. There was too much mess, too much or not enough open space ready for use; ground too zealously or not well enough cleared. He knew nothing more, hardly anything at all, than at the start of the day, and yet he had tried to apply the principles he'd heard from the old man ... listen to the belly, the belly, the belly! ... and yet nothing. Just a soulless clearing of bush, little better than a bulldozer could have done. He wished that, in one stroke, he could put back the land as he'd found it, with its leaves, its trees, everything that made the earth alive, since *he* was incapable of giving it anything whatsoever. It was dirty, ugly. Where there should have been a space there stood an abandoned-looking tree. Where there should have been a rock or a stump there was a big space like a desert. It was all like that. Jacques picked up his knife, took a few steps as if to return to his task – and collapsed. Face down on the earth he lay, floored by fatigue and disheartenment. For long minutes he made not the slightest movement. He was still conscious; he was almost weeping. He *was* weeping really but no tears flowed; it was happening inside his body and his heart. When Jacques sensed he was losing consciousness, he did not resist, he let himself go and imagined he was dying and that seemed to him good.

When he regained consciousness, the sun was already beginning to descend; it must have been three o'clock in the afternoon. He remained sprawling there in the dirt. He grabbed some handfuls of dead leaves and flung them over his body; he closed his eyes and tried to push his face as deeply as he could into the earth, his hands frantically scrabbling for twigs or anything else he could consume. He rolled his body until it was stopped by a stump; he pushed his fingers deep down into the soil and pulled out a handful, soil mixed with tiny bits of roots, and smeared this in his hair. He rolled again, back the other way, to where he was before; he gathered some stones, putting the little ones in his mouth and keeping the others in his hands. Through squirming about like this, like someone who's lost their mind, he found himself at the edge of the space he'd cleared. He stayed there a moment before raising his head. He looked around himself and spotted his bag, which had a salutary effect and brought him back to his senses. He got up, took the bag off the branch, and dug out his tobacco.

All that night he slogged on with the same work, the same actions, cutting, trimming, tearing down, burning the herbage and leaves, making piles of cut wood and uprooted stumps. All that night he cleared the bush, as bold and steady as if he'd slept a whole night, as if the plan of work were crystal clear in his mind. It was nothing like that really; Jacques was cutting pretty randomly, letting his strokes be driven more by the weight of the knife than by a true intention. He was too discouraged, he no longer believed enough in what he was doing to be able to do it with any thought. At times he even wanted to give it all up and go running back, in hopes of somehow finding his way to the main road, the one that passed near his home. At other times, though, he discovered a sense of elation, confident, reassured, as he recalled the old man's words, feeling certain, this time, he would perfectly apply his instructions. His exertions would then become smooth and precise, untiring. Throughout the night, these contrasting feelings alternated in Jacques' mind, but in the end it was despair that prevailed; he no longer really believed in anything.

Jacques cut down one last grove of lantanas and found himself standing in front of a perfectly cleared space. He stopped and beheld the ensemble of firewood, harmoniously laid-out trunks, neatly arranged stumps, remains of fireplaces. Everything as it might be in a man-made garden. He sat down, quite amazed. This shamba was perfect; it was what he'd been dreaming of since he'd left his house two days before. Nothing remained in excess, nothing seemed missing, everything expressed a perfect balance between symmetry and disorder ... Jacques looked more carefully; he couldn't believe what he was seeing – or what he now comprehended: this clearing was his own, the very one he'd rejected the last evening he'd returned home.

What surprised him was not that he'd rediscovered his first clearing after hacking so wildly as he'd been doing from the start; for he'd evidently moved through a large circle that had brought him back to where he'd started. No, what surprised him and left him speechless was that he was so pleased with this shamba; he liked it where before he'd seen only a sorry mess. After two days of cutting and hauling, two days of seeking, of questioning, of despair, he had come back to the place where he'd started. New eyes and a new heart let him appreciate the true worth of this first plot of land, the one where he'd worked regularly, calmly, each day, each week, and was at last, now, at peace with himself.

Vigil

She stayed always in her own country. Her country was a mysterious island that was said to lie in the direction of the rising sun. On this island dwelt many women reputed to be beautiful and generous. They lived in homes scattered far from each other, either alone or with a female relative. The island was generous also. Nature there was never angry; it's said that during cyclones the waves never came past the line of coconut palms along the beach and the winds and rains never tore away the roofs from the houses. To this island the white man never came. The Great Mariner passed close by; the sun was shining high and bright, but he saw nothing, heard nothing. Night and day, the sailors keep seeking. They all journey in search of fires where food is cooking. But their thoughts are not beautiful and they remain blind and sad. Before the women's eyes the sailors pass by and return homewards, to the open sea. And she, she stayed in her own country, and her reputation spread. It reached the Man of Néo. The question of her marriage interested everyone, for this young woman welcomed no proposals.

So the Chief of Néo says, 'I will go to see her.'

And he enters his roundhouse, he tugs an assegai from the bundle, digs his hand into his basket to pull out a beautiful red turban. He takes a feather crest from the case lodged in the bamboo canes of the wall. Finally, before departing, he makes sure he has a small packet of black powder made from fungus and a packet of green powder that comes from ferns. He takes as well a supply of mangrove fruit for the journey. He reaches his boat and embarks. And the wind drives him, without haste, without waves. His route leads him to the village. At one end of the central avenue he preens himself and then whistles to make his presence known. Everything is silent; both the forest and the shore seem lifeless. The birds have all vanished; perhaps they've abandoned him. The young girl's mother looks up, but the girl herself just carries on weaving a mat. With her face to the mountains, she turns her back to the Man of Néo.

And the mother says, 'Look who comes there. Who's this traveller? In which village did he grow up so handsome? Is he from a place we don't know, is he from one of those valleys we've never been to, or has he sprung from our thoughts?'

And then she speaks to him: 'Someone travels and where is he from? Whence comes this handsome traveller?'

'That's me, I guess, the Chief of Néo.'

'And what have you come to say? What do you bring? Your heart?'

'I come to hear your household's bidding.'

'That's good. Wait a moment. I'm going to talk to those children over there who are weaving mats and counting shells.'

She goes off to speak to her daughter, who hasn't moved a step from where she was or slowed down in her work. The girl replies, 'I don't know this man and I'm staying here. I'm waiting for the Man of Néawé.'

'That's fine,' concludes the Man of Néo. 'I only came to offer an exchange of gifts.'

And he disappeared from the avenue. Next day found him on the sea, untroubled. The days after that, he was back at home, still untroubled, getting on with his life. And no one asked him where he'd been or why he hadn't brought back the girl. It was only an exchange he'd thrown to fortune in a dream.

By the Edge of the Sea

And there, in his country, they still speak of the island and especially of that girl who refused the Man of Néo and wove mats while she was talked about, awaiting some chief from Néawé.

And her reputation, still spreading, reached at last the ear of the Chief of Wénaro, who lived a carefree life in his village of fisherfolk. The Chief of Wénaro was a man whose mere thought could bring forth fish and pacify men. His vision was not limited by either night or distance; was so acute that one day he saw the island in the distance and decided he should go.

'What was the Chief of Néo trying to do?' he says to the villagers. 'He's not one of those who fish on the reef, who know how to use the fur of the flying fox or to dig up the black powder of fungi. He knows only the rising and setting of the sun. He remains alone. I will go to see this girl. I'm going to find some provisions and get ready my pirogue. In the middle of the pools I'll seek only the little crayfish; I'll pull gently on their antennae, whistling to them, and they'll let themselves come into my hand. When I leave I'll give the village what's left from my catch so that while I'm away they'll have no fear of hunger. And to any who want to follow me I say that tomorrow the swell will drag their bodies upon the reef, for there's passage for only one pirogue through the pass that leads where my eyes have seen the avenue up to the roundhouse.'

Next day, he goes into his own roundhouse and comes out with everything he needs. To his brother he gives the remaining spears and assegais, for, he says, where he's going he'll have no need of mementos ... and, with that, he sets off to find his pirogue, which awaits him in another cove. The going is easy, the wind is blowing in the right direction, and the Chief of Wénaro fears nobody; his hour has come. The Chief of Néo was punier than him and did not go with the same thoughts. He walks along the road a long time, without stopping; he'll eat at

Néawé, where his pirogue is waiting. He gets there, and before he goes any further he eats, and after that he lies down. Soon his thoughts have journeyed so far that he is no longer where he lies. Soon the names that he knows no longer match the valleys or mountains that he sees. The man is upright, his face blackened by thick smoke billowing from a fire made of bad wood, and around him he can make out a roundhouse and further away some more houses and further still the sea and then nothing. A bit later he's leaning against a tree that, like him, is blackened by smoke and he sees, powerless to do anything, the man peel away from the tree and walk and let out a whistling sound.

Now two women appear. He doesn't know them, but they do seem to know him, for they show no sign of surprise. They're the mother and the daughter. The mother takes a look at the man and then speaks to her daughter: 'You see this traveller? Is he not handsome? I'm going to talk to him and see what he says.'

But the girl stops her mother. 'You're not thinking what you're saying. That man wouldn't know how to come all the way here.'

The mother replies, 'The Man of Néo has already been here and as soon as he listened to you he was gone again. Where does this one come from? Why would you want to just drive him away?' And she turns to the man who has the same walk as the Man of Wénaro: 'Have you come so far that your face has turned so black and cannot change back?'

'It's me, the Man of Wénaro, I tell you.'

'I don't know him,' says the girl. 'I won't go following after a sleeping shade whose thoughts couldn't come here with him. I await the son of Néawé – the man who is descended from the rocks, from a line of a hundred men and a hundred women.'

'I'm waiting,' says the shade. 'I think I'll just go back with what I brought.'

By the Edge of the Sea

The Chief of Wénaro is still on the ground where he lay down to rest before leaving and when the spear prods him awake he can't work out what he's doing there. The pirogue has gone; he no longer knows where he is. He hits the road again and he walks and walks and gets lost for a long, long time and all the villagers are waiting and one by one they leave, because there's nothing left for them. And when at last the man finds his way back to the village he finds just a handful of men and women who don't know who he is.

The words were flowing from the storyteller's lips and still they kept coming. As the story got longer he took breaths at longer and longer intervals. He walked slowly up and down with little steps, as if to give rhythm in this way to the characters' breath, ten, fifteen steps one way and then as many the other way, with always the fire in the middle, lighting up his face and lighting up his bare skin so it shone in the night. He looked at no one, only the sky far above him, and the tale continued.

The woman was waiting for the Chief of Néawé. All this time, that man was in his own country, his own village, and knew nothing. And yet his ears and his thoughts were pulling his heart beyond what he could see, far over the land, far over the sea. He lived without want or need. Each day was his sunshine. Each day was his joy. But by now the young woman was exhausting the patience of her mother, who could see she was becoming like all the other women on their island; she feared her lost for any man, since none had been able to carry her away in his dream. And the mother, who longed only for her daughter to be taken, could not find any ship, for her mind had not the power to travel. This country remained the most lovely and its women the most desirable. They had chosen their queen, yet those who chanced to pass by saw nothing of her because their hearts were already taken. But before the Man of

Néawé learnt anything of this woman in her country, there stumbled upon the island the Man of M., who came, yelling, to steal the woman and who, faced by her beauty and her silence, looked her up and down and lusted to chuck a stone in her belly. Till all of a sudden the Man of M. falls on his knees, then his nose, and soon the leaves cover him and he never goes back to his village, wherever that may be, and nobody weeps for him and now his body has disappeared without trace; his face is forgotten, so disgusting it was.

At last the day came when the Man of Néawé knew he must speak. He said, 'I'm going to go to the country my blood comes from, to the place of my uncles.'

He asked the pirogue-builders to take up their knives and stakes in order to cut down a tree and make a big pirogue to carry him with all his gifts and victuals to the other side of the reef, to the country where the girl is waiting for him. But the pirogue-builders' work was not a success and the boat sank to the bottom of the sea when he boarded it. Everyone wept. The man said nothing and slipped away for a whole night. Upon his return he decides to go on foot. He walks, he walks, and when he thinks he's arrived somewhere he looks around but he can see nothing. So he sets off along another route he thinks he's found. He forges on and on, deeper and deeper that way, but still he finds nothing and now he too wants to weep.

When at last he's home he says to the villagers, 'We're going to climb up to the high forest to look for a suitable tree.'

And together they found a giant houp that was strong, good, and straight. They had a big discussion about it and concluded, 'That's it, we've found the long pirogue he wants. For now, let's just allow the day to pass; another one will come and then we'll come back to take away the tree.'

Everyone returns home and stays there to await the destined day. When the Man of Néawé gives the nod, they say, 'Tomorrow we'll climb up to the forest and cut down our long pirogue.'

When they've slept, the new day comes and they have another discussion: 'We can cut it down all right, but on this rough, steep path it will be hard, even impossible, to transport it.'

Someone else says, 'Let's forget about that tree. Let's go back there and have a think.'

They all troop back. At length they make a decision: 'You see all these trees? We're going to tie these lianas on to them and then each of us will pull as best he can. The forest will come down and the tree will come with it. Let's get on with it. Just forget about the tree and soon we'll find it down there near the village.'

Once the lianas are attached, they pull, and ho and ho and the forest is tugged, but it stays where it is. And one of the lianas snaps, is retied, and breaks again and now all the lianas keep snapping.

'We're not doing too well. Let's come back tomorrow after we've had some food and a good sleep.'

The next day comes and the same thing happens – the lianas are all new but again they break and the men fall down, one after another, and the Man of Néawé falls down too, and he doesn't think he's going to get anywhere, for this forest is so well rooted. He says, 'Let's leave this forest be; it will not provide my pirogue. We've wasted a lot of strength and food for nothing. Let's forget it. You go home. I'm going to venture a bit further.'

That night the Man of Néawé didn't sleep; his mind's eye far away, he wept silently. He had no means to reach the girl. He thought he would never receive the gift of her maternal relatives. He knew no way to succeed in getting there. And he was dismayed that he was so heavy, that his spirit was so bound. He told himself that he could do nothing more now, that he should go to sleep. He went a little way distant and with some leaves and some wood he made himself a shelter and he lay down under it to sleep awhile. Soon he had a dream – that was populated by a rat and a man, a turtle and children. In his sleep, he could see that the rat was in his house.

'I'm going to take a trip to the reef,' thought the rat one day. 'I miss the spray and the salt these days.' And he went to sleep. In the morning he cooked a yam, put it in his provisions basket, embarked on a length of sugar cane, and this boat whistled out to sea.

Then the kingfisher arrives on the scene. 'Tell me, ratty, where are you going?'

'To the reefs.'

'Let's go together.'

'Come then.'

They're sailing faster now. The rat takes his basket out of its recess and asks the kingfisher, 'What have you brought?'

'Erm, I have nothing.'

So the rat shares what he has and says, 'We'll eat together, but if a crumb falls into the bottom of the boat don't pick it up.'

Soon they're eating and the kingfisher keeps dropping lots of crumbs. When the meal is finished, the bird really wants those crumbs and with a quick dart he beaks them up. But he also pierces the bottom of the skiff, the boat sinks, and though the kingfisher can fly away the rat is left behind. He swims and meets a shark.

'Hey, please take me! Please carry me to dry land!'

'Ratty,' says the shark, 'don't you know that on the shore they have their spears ready to run me through? So I can't take you. I just can't do it.'

The rat swims on and meets all sorts of fishes. He begs them one after another but the response is always the same: 'Don't you know they have spears ready?'

By the Edge of the Sea

'Hey, turtle, good turtle!' he calls out when he sees the turtle. 'Please carry me to the shore.'

'Sit yourself on my neck,' she replies.

So there he sits and the turtle swims towards the shore. When they get there the rat jumps off and runs away. But the people of the coast, from behind the coconut palms, have spotted this man and the turtle and they rush out to grab her. They pull her on to dry land and take her away, laughing as they go, to their village. The rat is well away, hiding in the undergrowth. The people go and present the turtle to the chief.

Then everyone goes to bed. In the morning the chief summons his people: 'Today I tell you all to go and gather vegetables and this evening we'll have a feast in which we'll eat this here turtle. Hah, that man is clever to have got the turtle to carry him to the shore! Our spears have no fish but we have turtle for tonight. Let's go, let's go!'

They entrust the turtle to the children and all hurry off into the plantations. In his sleep, the Chief of Néawé wondered who was the kingfisher, who was the rat, who was the turtle, and what this story meant, as he slept on without hope of ever meeting anyone.

Near the middle of the day, that man, the rat, makes his way back to find the turtle.

'Get ready,' he tells her. 'I'm going to try something.'

He sets off to find Wawa.

'May I ask you to sing a few songs and to dance?'

And Wawa sings: '*Koa, koa, koa.*'

'Your song is no good!' cries the rat, and off he goes to seek out different birds. But none of their songs is any better. Then he speaks to Kaoupoésoa: 'Ah, just the man! May I ask you to sing and dance?'

Kaoupoésoa sang: '*U, u, u.*' He sang admirably. He danced admirably. The children soon let go of the turtle's rope to go and listen to Kaoupoésoa's singing and watch him dancing. Meanwhile the rat creeps forward, nibbles the turtle's bonds, cuts them with his teeth.

'Quick, flee away!' he says. 'You can rest once you're back in the sea.'

The turtle hauls herself in haste, no looking back, till she reaches the water's edge and takes to the open sea.

The rat goes to find Kaoupoésoa. 'Thank you very much for the dance you've been giving rhythm to and dancing for me. You can take a rest now.' And the dance stops.

The children say, 'That's the end of the dancing. Let's go back to that turtle that's going to be our dinner.'

They found only a few bits of cord. They were standing there in surprise when the chief came back with his people. Everyone put down their load – yams, taro, sugar cane to eat that evening with the turtle. They hadn't seen the dancing or heard the singing … but, seeing no sign of the turtle, they asked, 'Children, the turtle you were guarding here this morning, where is she?'

'Erm, we don't know. She went home a while ago.'

The village then explodes with anger. But soon everyone calms down.

'Let's put together our food and eat.'

The rat, standing high, thus the man, saw all. He headed back to the beach.

And the Man of Néawé wakes up feeling pleased and goes outside. What he's understood and what's made him feel so sure of himself is that the rat was *him*: ready to depart but unable to find his way; getting lost and always returning in tears. He's realised that the other characters in his dream were his mistakes and at last his success. The kingfisher represented his first mistake; he had come and sunk the pirogue too visible for such a journey. The fish had refused to carry him, for fish will die on land; they are prisoners of their element – as he was prisoner of his mind until he went to sleep. Finally, the turtle was his salvation; she had managed to get away. She'd helped the rat get back to the land; at risk of death she'd come out of the sea. The turtle is free to go where she will. The Man of Néawé has understood how he ought to be and which path he has to take.

And so he jumps up and says, 'I'm going to take the way that leads to the country I am from, the way that leads to my maternal uncles. No need of a pirogue for that. I'll take the path from behind the village.'

He ties around his forehead some heavy lengths of money, and he takes a sling as well, and he fills his hand with stones. The stones when he throws them leap along the path to guide him where he wants to go.

'It's me, auntie!'

'Who?'

'Who besides me would be guided here by stones?'

And the mother is barged out of the way by the woman who has waited so long and has seen too many bad men. She's nervous and her eyes are no longer sure what they see.

She says, 'Come in, man.'

'No, let me go first to the side alley so I can put down on the rocks this burden which is pounding my forehead.'

'Mother, he's going to leave. His spirit is still heavy. He believes that his journey is ended; but I have yet to be taken. So I'm leaving with him. It's time that he had me with him.'

And away the two of them go. The journey takes some time and one dark night along the way a strange man snatches the woman away and beats her and takes her inside his house. And the Chief of Néawé arrives back at his village and wakes up.

'They tell me I'm alone – quite alone. Haven't I lost something on the way? Hasn't something been stolen from me? So I gather the men and in one fell swoop we smash down the trees blocking the way, and with one blow I smash this man and tear off his member. Someone tells me, "The one who came with you, she's burying his member in the earth and then she'll come to live with you."'

And the two of them, in their village, in their roundhouse, they live together a very long time.

The old man, the storyteller, stopped his story. He allowed a few minutes to pass in which not a word could be heard and even the breath of all the listeners could barely be discerned. Only the sounds of the forest and the shore a few metres away, and the crackling of the fire, broke the silence. Still immersed in the tale and the voice of the storyteller, we found ourselves suddenly alone.

'That's it, I've told it,' he said at last. 'That's how we used to choose our wives. You would sleep beside the fire and everything would happen while you slept, as if it was a dream, but it wasn't really a dream. It's not like that these days; things are different. But that's the way that I found a wife; that's the way you all came to be born. Now all that's finished. I've told you this story so that you won't forget. Even if you no longer do these things, you won't forget; you have to know, you young ones, what we old ones used to do to find a wife and to give life. But now it's time to sleep.'

Everyone got up, and first the young children ran noisily to the roundhouses that you could make out around us in the darkness. Then the less young, their parents, walking more quietly, talking in low voices, but they too were hurrying. The fire was dim and it was starting to get cold. I stayed a little while longer to make the most of the night and the silence, so special for me, used to the incessant noise of the city. The old man was still there too. I watched him. I'd got to know him a bit because we'd come in the same car for this annual gathering of all the

Christians of the region, which coincides with Easter. He was sitting very near the embers, his eyes nearly closed. But he was not sleeping; perhaps he was thinking of his wife who'd died a few years before.

Market Women

Very early in the morning, well before sunrise, two women rise from their beds. They get up at the same hour, in the same fishing village, separated by no more than five hundred metres of beach and coconut palms. They have both slept very little. This morning they have much to do.

One of them has been kept awake by her child. A very young child, barely eighteen months old. He's a boy, puny and helpless right now, but his mother knows that one day he'll be big and strong and he will look after her. Throughout the night she tried to soothe him by singing him a lullaby. Sometimes she dozed off at the same time as he did. But soon enough his cries would wake her and she would resume her lullaby. All the mothers in the village know these songs. They speak of the simple things of life; they speak of these things as they might be seen and understood with the heart of a child. In these songs the departure of the fishermen became a heroic expedition in which the nets were thrown to catch not fish but monsters from the bottom of the ocean. The frail boats became gigantic ships armed with a thousand warriors, each one of them more valorous than the next. The fisherman was no longer a mere fisherman, but an invincible hero. The lullabies told then, as if the story were being sung back to front, of the waiting of those who'd stayed in the village: the women, the mothers, the girls, who as they did their usual chores would keep glancing anxiously to the horizon. Finally, they told of the delight and the rejoicing when the fishermen-heroes set foot on the sand and you could see that none of them was missing: not one of them had died; no father or husband or brother had disappeared. All of this the songs told with soft and magical words. The magic was conjured also by the slow rhythm and by the mother's whispering voice, barely audible, as if breathed from the ocean. In the child's heart this magic transformed the warlike deeds into benign ones, in which the iron and the blood were dispelled and only love remained. So well the magic worked that, little by little, all cares left the child, who would always end up falling sleep, if only for a few minutes. Then the mother would hum a lullaby, another lullaby, one that would tell perhaps of the endless journeys of the great seabirds.

This woman who's been awake a long time, who's sung and contemplated throughout the night, and dozed off several times, who felt a quiver of fear whenever she heard on the beach the noise of something she couldn't see through the fronds of the young coconut palms – this woman now has to prepare her three baskets and tidy up the disarray left from the evening before and the night in the house. She will take care not to wake her husband, who's been asleep for a while, after a long night of fishing. Then she will venture on to the beach to gather some seaweed still green, still moist and salty, with which to line the bottom of her baskets.

Her husband did come back. He came back after fishing all night with his two companions. Upon his return they looked at each other, both of them tired but glad to be together again, with the little one at last asleep.

The other woman who stayed awake nearly all the night sang as well. She didn't sing for her child, though, because she doesn't yet have one. She didn't sing a lullaby, because you don't sing lullabies any more to a man. All evening and right up to midnight, she made herself ready and tidied the house. She took her time to groom herself. She combed her long black hair with her old turtleshell comb, sitting in front of a little mirror that reflected her big black eyes. She draped a cotton wrap around her hips and her breasts and tied it at her left shoulder with a small flat knot. Dressed like this, she tidied up the two rooms of the house, which stood among the other houses of wood and woven palm leaves, a few metres from the sea, in the shade of the coconut palms. She tidied the veranda too. The task was simple: neither in the house nor on the veranda where she laid out the mat on which she's sitting are there many possessions. A mattress on the floor, a chair, and a trunk in one room. In the other, a table, a few chairs, a chest of drawers for the crockery, and a wardrobe. Now she watches the sea. Night has fallen. There is no noise except the washing of the waves and the swaying of the coconut palms.

When her man arrives back, she will be there, on the veranda, already as close to him as she can be. Just a few metres before her, almost at her feet, the waves wash and wet the sand. She's so close to them that she gets a fleeting sensation of feeling the water on her feet. The water is still tepid; the heat stored up during the day will not completely dissipate till the middle of the night – till nearly as late an hour as when he usually returns. To the right she can make out between the coconut palms a few lights from the village. She does not watch them for long. She turns all her attention back to the ocean, the horizon, so far away out there. Although it's night, she can see by the grace of the full moon the spot where any moment now the boat and her husband will slowly come into view.

At last her husband is there, in front of her, lightly clothed and wet with salty water, now chilling him. She takes him by the hand and leads him indoors. Once they're in the room, the one that serves as their bedroom, she undresses him and speaks to him. She tells him about her afternoon and evening, what she saw and heard while she was awaiting him, sitting alone on the veranda. He's tired, she knows. So while he sits there naked, hardly moving at all, she dries him using simply her hands and her mouth. At the same time she sings. Short verses of two lines followed by a longer chorus. It's into this chorus that she puts all her passion, her love, her desire, the desire to love and be loved. Yet her touch and her voice are also to comfort him. She knows that fishing by night is not entirely a pleasure, so she wants to soothe him. And little by little her caresses and her kisses upon her husband's skin, upon her husband's body, arouse her desire. She communicates this desire to him in turn. Soon, as they lie one against the other, she will with practised fingers unknot her wrap and they will both be naked. He now lulled by her song and her caresses; she brimming with desire to give herself, to receive his force and his love, to feel in her every tissue his secret joy to find her still awake even though the night is so advanced. They will cling tight together, forget the village and the sea, and tell themselves that his every return from sea will be like this, for many a long year. The moon watching over them, they will at last go to sleep. She for a few hours only. But the waiting for her man's presence, and the seawater that her skin will have drunk, will have brought her as much rest and strength to face the new day as will the two hours of sleep that remain to her.

Early this morning, she got up at nearly the same moment as the other woman, no more than a few hundred metres down the beach. She does the same things as her. She goes to the fishpond where her husband left the fish. She washes them, prepares three baskets with seaweed that tastes and smells of the sea.

When at last the sun appears, two women are already at the market. Sitting one beside the other, they know each other, they speak together. In front of them, on a mat, they have put their fish. The fish are the same: almost the same number, almost the same size, almost the same varieties. All of them will have been bought before the morning's end. One of the women has her child in her arms: he sleeps, he wakes, he sleeps again. The other woman, whose bare shoulders you can see – and for a moment, when she shifts her position, the top of a thigh – she doesn't yet have a child. Perhaps without thinking, perhaps because her instinct compels it, she passes her hand at regular intervals over a belly still flat and firm.

By the Edge of the Sea – I

At the tag end of summer I'd got into the habit, around eight o'clock in the evening, of walking along the large bay that skirts the coast to the south of the city. Some nights the wind blowing off the sea is so violent that it's almost impossible to maintain a steady pace. You have to stop for a little rest every seven or eight steps along certain stretches that you have to cover very slowly till you reach the shelter provided by three successive rows of coconut palms. After that, thanks to an inexplicable softening of the wind, you can resume walking at the pace you started out with. With the wind come smells that vary with the tides. If the tide is right in, the smell of the sea is so weak, so diffuse, you can hardly detect it. But if you go for a walk at low water during the great spring tides the whole coral platform will be exposed and the stench will be strong, almost too strong. The iodine reaches right into your stomach and for people with unusually sensitive guts the impulse to vomit can quickly become overwhelming. These individuals tend not to go out on the coast at low tide. I am blessed not to have such a sensitive stomach; in fact I love this smell, the smell of the sea, the shellfish, the seaweed, and mixed with all that the smell of crabs crushed under stones the children have blithely been turning over all day long, imagining themselves to be great fishermen. Neither does the wind alarm me. To struggle against the wind in the course of a long, solitary walk is one of the satisfactions I

By the Edge of the Sea – I

get from these late-night excursions.

During my walks I had noticed, on the flank of the hill that runs alongside the road, the tops of lots of banana leaves jutting out from the undergrowth of shrubs and bushes. At first I thought they must belong to wild banana trees – or else to pandanus palms, whose leaves from a distance resemble those of the huge banana trees that can be found in ancient, long-abandoned shambas. But quickly I rejected this notion, for pandanus does not grow in this part of the country, and neither are there any wild bananas. For the latter to grow, someone must first come and plant some bananas, and then abandon them, giving the shoots free rein to grow and multiply, or to die. But people rarely abandon a banana tree they've planted. So I came to the obvious conclusion that what I'd seen was evidence of a Melanesian smallholding. From then on, I observed this hillside more closely and I spotted other things, other clues that convinced me that up there, behind a row of bushes and leucaena and gaïac trees, lay one or more shambas that were being carefully maintained by Kanak. As well as the banana leaves that had first caught my attention, I could clearly make out the tops of some support poles of the kind used to train the growth of yam plants while the roots, the edible tubers, swell and stretch underground, sheltered from sight and the many dangers that menace all existence on the surface. And if you looked carefully you would see the gap in the vegetation's outline caused by the cutting of a small clearing to make a shamba – just there, on the hillside, a matter of metres from the road and the cars, from the passers-by, walkers, and joggers. That was not all. At regular intervals along the road a number of paths seemed to plunge through the undergrowth directly towards the summit of the hill. About every fifty metres a little gap in the bushes betrayed to the experienced eye the beginning of a pathway hardly big enough for a man to pass through; the one that most drew my attention looked as though it had been deliberately concealed. I imagined that all these paths led to clearings – small ones of twenty by twenty metres at most, to judge by the gaps in the vegetation which I could see from the road. No peasant farmer, no gardener would be keen for strangers seeking communion with nature to treat his path as a hiking or running route. I understood perfectly that that was why the proprietors had tried to hide their paths and gardens from the eyes of passers-by.

To begin with, when I got home I would forget these gardens and these paths. I would spend a moment in the bathroom and then pick up a book to get me to sleep. After a few days, a few walks, when I was sure that all I suspected did truly exist, I ceased to need the book. I would lie stretched out on the bed, naked, letting my imagination run along the path, reach the clearing, and populate the shamba with the various species I knew would be planted there. Never did I imagine this shamba in broad daylight, flooded by sunshine in crystal clarity. I would see it exclusively in the dead of night, by the sole light of the moon, when in my dream she wished to come out. Its borders were never well defined, nor were the shapes of the trees or the leaves or the colours of the ground. Nearly everything was grey or brown. The only colour that stood out was green and only the banana trees and the long stalks of sugar cane had the privilege of retaining this lovely colour. The leaves of the wild trees that fringed the shamba were faintly stained with light, but never in my dreams or my wandering thoughts before sleep did I picture them in their true colours.

Before going to sleep, when my mind had ceased to stray upon that hillside, I said to myself, I promised myself, that the next day or whenever the opportunity came I would go and investigate more closely what substance there was to my imaginings. How large were these clearings, these shambas? Whither

By the Edge of the Sea – I

led the paths that at night directed my dreams? And then the next day the promise would be forgotten; I no longer saw any reason to go wandering through the bushes at risk of looking like an eccentric if any walkers stumbled upon me. Up till the evening, up till nightfall, I was an amnesiac. But when the sun vanished over the horizon the mists of forgetfulness evaporated and I would be haunted anew by the thought of those clearings in the bush. Sometimes a lapse of several days separated my walks, but when I again approached one of the paths the impulse to follow it would take hold of me, the impulse to plunge into the undergrowth and emerge into some other space. I resisted it, telling myself I had no right to pursue this desire. The shambas were nothing to do with me; I had no reason to go there except a kind of tourist's whim; nothing tangible justified my presence in such places. So I would continue on my way without even pausing. But something was telling me that I needed no reason to go and see what people did the other side of the road. The mere desire to go there and feel good – for I knew I'd feel good there, I had many times before spent long hours inside a Kanak garden, so distinctively arranged, and I'd always felt my soul at peace – this simple desire was enough by itself to motivate my presence up there. On the other hand, I was afraid of meeting or being caught there by the owner, and that was enough to block the fulfilment of my desire for several weeks. But desire and love are more powerful than fear of the other, and I was propelled by precisely these two marvellous forces. One evening, therefore, I left home knowing that I was going to follow the first path I came to. When I arrived near the sea, at half past eight, there was no moon, but I knew perfectly the positions of the various paths. After a half-hour's walking I ducked without hesitating into a kind of natural tunnel that covered the start of a dirt path. I had to push aside a few branches, which flicked back in place behind me to reconceal the entrance. From the road it would be impossible for a passer-by to see me walking under the trees.

That first time I did not stay long. Upon arriving at the edge of the shamba, which I was surprised to find was much further from the road than I was expecting, I stood motionless to observe the place. I gave it a quick once-over with my eyes, without dwelling on any spot or any plant in particular. I think that fear was my uppermost feeling then. The fear of being caught there, certainly, but equally a fear of the place and its magic. I remembered all the stories of demons, of phantoms, of spirits that are supposed to come and bother intruders and that I'd been told about many times during my stays on the islands among Melanesians. In a confused way I felt afraid that these stories, which serve to delight at the same time as to frighten children, might in part be true and that right then, at the moment I penetrated into this human space, something might happen. Something supernatural in a place so close to nature and its often uncontrollable forces. At last, I managed to suppress this rather silly fear and I sat down on the ground at the very spot I had emerged from the path. I stayed like that maybe twenty minutes and then, without hesitation, without one last look at the clearing as a whole, I got up, turned my back on the banana trees and sugar cane, and walked quickly back along the path to the road. Thirty minutes later I was home.

There came in these last days of summer a terrible resurgence of heat. In the daytime the mercury in the thermometer passed the thirty-degree mark. Happily, in the evening it would inevitably rain. Between eight and ten o'clock the downpour would beat down on the whole city, which sat at the foot of a long chain of mountains extending far away northwards. Each time I arrived at the edge of the shamba I was soaked. There was no way I was going to light a fire to dry myself. Not that the place didn't lend itself to doing that, quite the contrary, but

By the Edge of the Sea – I

I feared that the remains of a fire would, the next day, betray my presence to the shamba's owner, who unstintingly came here each day. Of that I felt certain, for on each of my visits I noticed small changes. One time it was a few extra supports planted on the ridge of soil shaped for the yams; other times a few stalks of sugar cane had been cut or some banana leaves had been gathered up and piled at the foot of one of the trees. Bit by bit, these little clues brought to life for me the routine and work of the gardener in the clearing. From that I even began to picture this individual. I'm not exactly sure why, but after four visits I was convinced that the person who came every day to work there a few hours – two or three, certainly no more than three – was a woman. Evidently an older woman. There was so much care and gentleness, so much peace and maternalness, if I may call it so, that it could not be a man or someone young who had created this garden. One afternoon, I was passing in my car on the road between the water and the hill and I immediately spotted some smoke rising above the trees. Someone was in the shamba. It was a chance to see if my intuition was correct. But something prevented me stopping the car on the road verge. I realised at that moment that I would never have the courage to go to the shamba in broad daylight and meet this woman. I wanted to keep that space devoid of any human presence except my own. I was behaving there like someone from the beyond, who was there, yes, but as if suspended in the air: I was not contributing to the place in any way. As if the shamba were able to do everything by itself. I did not want to see with my own eyes that it could be useful to something other than simply the pleasure of the gaze and the spirit, or the peace of the soul and the heart. I did not wish to know that it produced something other than stillness and serenity. Okay, I'm not just a sweet dreamer who's oblivious of social reality. A shamba is a productive space that serves first and foremost an economic purpose. That more than anything else. It must produce supplementary provisions for a Melanesian family who will likely be living in town on a feeble salary, if they have one at all, insufficient to buy all the food needed for maybe seven or eight people. Unsurprising, therefore, was the painstaking care routinely brought to this shamba. The city is full of such shambas. The slightest bit of hillside is a patchwork of squares bristling with bananas, yams, taro, potatoes, sugar cane, and sometimes even maize and clumps of citronella. They nourish a population ever more numerous who find it hard to get work that's properly remunerated. In this way Kanak families are colonising the tiny green spaces of the city in an odd sort of reversal of this country's recent history. This shamba near the sea was really no different, but I feared that meeting its owner would take away from it some of the magic I felt there at night when, sitting on the ground, I took in the shapes and the smells that made the place almost a living being.

I knew that even at night I had to behave carefully so that no one the next day would suspect my nocturnal presence. I avoided wandering about among the yam plants. I took great care not to break the branches of shrubs that had been left growing in the spaces between the vegetable patches. I generally just sat in a corner, not always the same one, and observed. My gaze went from one point to another of the shamba without my trying to guide it in any particular way. My eyes would alight somewhere and stay there till something drew them elsewhere. Sometimes I closed my eyes and listened like that to the thousand sounds of the shamba. With practice I was able to name the sounds, knowing what produced them and where in the space around me they came from. I would then let my mind wander, away from the shamba, back to the coast, whence the road led me back home or to places where I'd once lived, either recently or long ago. Or I would try to allow a space to open

By the Edge of the Sea – I

within me; the place lent itself to that admirably and I had to watch out I didn't fall asleep. Whatever I did, the hours spent in all these places were imbued with stillness and abundance. I would come back from them calmed and with my heart filled with beauty and peace.

One night, maybe the seventh or eighth I spent there, while I was taking shelter from some light rain under a clump of sugar cane, I heard someone coming along the path. I moved quickly from my shelter to hide in the wild bushes outside the shamba. After a few seconds I saw a woman emerge from the path. She had a machete in her right hand and a woven bag hung by its strap from her left shoulder. I watched her. She paused a moment to wipe the rainwater from her face, then she headed to another clump of sugar cane, pulled from it a few dry leaves, picked up from the ground some bits of dead wood, and right there, two or three steps away from me, between two big stones – with astonishing ease in the rain – she lit a fire. Not a big fire, not a fire intended to warm her up or even to dry her properly; no, a fire just adequate to dry her hands and above all to exude a pleasant, hard-to-define smell of earth, leaves, and wood which mixed with the smells coming from the sea so close by. For about half an hour she sat there doing nothing except tend her fire. When the fire died, she departed as discreetly as she had come. I waited a dozen minutes, time enough for her to get back to the road and well enough away, and then left my hiding place and the shamba. I'd guessed right; a woman was taking care of this garden and her presence was discernible. I was even quite proud of myself that I'd had this intuition. It seemed like evidence of my harmony with the space and with the one – with her – who was creating it.

The next day it did not rain, but I returned to the shamba in the evening as had been my custom for some weeks now. I emerged from the path at the same instant as the moon came out of a bundle of clouds that had concealed it throughout my walk. It lit up the whole of the clearing, leaving in shadow the precise area outside the borders of the shamba. I remembered the night before and the fire near the sugar cane. There was still a little pile of ashes between the two big stones, a few steps from a lovely clump of citronella I'd never noticed before. This time, standing there, at the entrance of this splendid shamba that I was getting to know very well and to love as if it were part of my own home, I couldn't decide where to sit down. I kept hesitating. I took a step or two in one direction, then changed my mind and headed another way towards a shrub that was dead and dry but still firmly rooted in the ground. And then, just as I was crouching down, the spot no longer seemed ideal. I turned round and round, seeking something, finding nothing. The shamba was slipping through my fingers; it was no longer speaking to me; I no longer understood it. I had a feeling then that I ought to leave.

Recrossing the clearing, I passed near the remains of the fire. For some reason it struck me that the best place to sit down was by these ashes. So I sat down on one of the stones. Slowly, my sense of peace returned. I began to breathe with softer breaths and became conscious of all the smells entering me through my nostrils and finding their way to my belly. There was a little wind; I heard it clearly now, stealing between the branches to reach me. It brought with it the many smells of a very low tide. Everything became like before. I felt good, at peace with myself, my soul in perfect communion with the place and through that with the entirety of nature. In my thoughts I thanked the old Melanesian woman who, without knowing it, had bestowed on me such a marvellous sense of well-being. I heard a noise behind me, I turned around – and there she was, looking at me.

She came forward. 'Don't move. I'm going to sit down

beside you to redo the fire.'

I could neither move nor reply, so surprised I was and so flustered that I'd been discovered. In an instant, I understood that she had been there a long time, since the very start, that she'd never been unaware of my nightly visits. She had always known that someone was coming there at night. How had she known? Simply from the many signs that in my ignorance I'd always left behind me: small imprints that soil softened by rain will preserve a long time, branches slightly bent, stones I'd dislodged on the path without even noticing them, and yet other signs that were nothing to me but had revealed to her not only the visitor's presence but his identity.

'With a fire you always feels better out here. Even if it's small and not very strong you can still make use of it. The youngsters when they come with me, they love to cook under the ashes some pieces of young yam. This evening I have nothing to cook, though, and it wasn't for cooking that I made the fire the other night.'

'You knew I was here that evening, didn't you? Was it for me that you lit it?'

'Of course I knew you were there, hiding in the bushes just behind me. You, you've never seen me though I've been close by nearly every night.'

She said that to tease me a little, to help break the ice between us.

'The fire, I made it for you,' she said, 'but I have the feeling you did not realise that.'

I had indeed never imagined that the flames, the heat, the smells were intended to invite me out of the bushes to join her in the warmth instead of staying cold in the rain. It was such a different attitude from what I would expect of a landowner who'd caught an intruder on their property. To think that this old Melanesian was as curious as me!

By the Edge of the Sea

We were sitting opposite each other, either side of the fire. For a time neither she nor I spoke. Sometimes we looked at each other and she would smile at me and then look away. I thought that if I was not going to apologise I should at least try to explain my repeated presence in her shamba. Poking the embers absent-mindedly with a piece of wood, I at last broke the silence.

'I did not wish to disturb or take anything. It's just that this place drew me. I could see the leaves and support poles from the road. Sometimes when I was passing on the road I saw smoke; so I came to see. When I'm here in the evening I feel great; I forget everything. It's as if I'm in another world, closer to nature and the sky. As if I'm part of nature. Even the first time, it was like that, so I came back. It was always like that. I came back nearly every night, just to feel so good. I come, I am here, because I love this place. I love the shapes, the colours, the sounds, the smells, everything that you've made here. I should have found you first and asked your permission, but at the start I couldn't, I dared not do that. Later it was too late, it had become impossible, I was coming here so often. For you the shamba isn't a place for dreaming. It's important – you need it for your family, for yourself, for goods to exchange. I know that and I'm so sorry if some nights I may have broken something. I've been walking about here as if it were a recreation ground. I feel embarrassed to be here with you, I shouldn't have been here, since it's your place and I didn't come and ask. But maybe you understand; it's so beautiful here, so peaceful, so silent, and at the same time so alive that, once I'd come here the first time, I couldn't forget it and needed to come back.'

What I was saying must have seemed rambling and well-nigh incomprehensible. It was both an explanation and an embarrassed description of my feelings; I was asking her to accept my apologies at the same time as I was asking her to let me come back. I may even have said that I'd like to come to work with her there from time to time.

'It's no problem,' she said to me. 'No problem at all. You did right to come here if it makes you feel good.' She allowed a few seconds to pass, perhaps a whole minute, and then she continued: 'You know, the soil is not very good here and things don't grow very well. I have other shambas over the other side of the hill. This one I keep up only because I love this spot, I really love to be near the sea. It's a bit like with you; it's to dream that I come here. I come, I trim the bushes, then I clear up, I burn some rubbish, I plant and transplant, and afterwards I sit down and relax. I think about nothing, I look around, or I think about my children and my elders. I let go of everything. It's worth doing the shamba just for that. It's normal. It doesn't matter what exactly you do, you feel good afterwards when you go home. I've watched you and seen how you behave a bit like me. You sit there and do nothing. Me too, I come here at night. I wait till everyone at home is asleep, then I pick up a torch and cross the hill to get here. That's how it was, the first time I saw you. I was coming to sit and rest awhile – and just as I was entering the shamba I spotted you. I stayed outside to watch you. Eventually you left and I left after you.'

She carried on talking like this for a long time, a very long time, using her own particular ways of phrasing things. I comprehended that was she talking to me about the harmony of her shamba, which was like that which should exist in life, so that between the two there is an exchange; one harmony reflects the other and helps it in turn be more harmonious and beautiful. Her speech contained long moments of silence which sometimes I broke with a few words and then she would resume talking and tell me things about nature, about her life, about life in general, about a way to plant such and such a plant which was like a way of doing anything, whether here or elsewhere.

She told me when she had planted her yams and with whom she'd done that, and why this shamba was the one she liked best, even though in the end it served no practical purpose. She talked for a long, long time, and I did so too, replying to her, forgetting how the hours were passing as I was carried along by the sounds and scents of the tide.

By the Edge of the Sea – II

If only he would lift his gaze from the ground. If he were to look in my direction, he would surely see me. Then he would come over to me and when we'd introduced ourselves, as custom demands, he would speak to me. He would ask me why I come here every day – whether the fishing is so interesting that one can devote so many hours to it as I do without getting bored. He would patiently await my reply and from this a proper conversation would begin between us. I've known for a long time how I shall respond to such a question; every morning for thirty days I've awaited him and he has come to walk along this turfy, shady footpath. He arrives from the east; I see him when he comes round the turning that takes you away from the road. He keeps his eyes down. He keeps his head lowered as well as his gaze, so much so that I get the impression he's looking for something on the ground and soon he will straighten up his head and body and walk normally, to make the most of the air and the sun. He walks quickly, though without doing a route march like so many of the people who frequent this lovely path by the water's edge. He must see nobody, either to the side or in front of him. He advances without paying attention to what's happening around him; a cyclist goes by at full tilt, misses him by less than a metre, and he doesn't react; some lads shoot their ball between his legs and he barely slows down to avoid stumbling.

By the Edge of the Sea

I'll simply tell him that fishing is often just an excuse to pass the time pleasurably, enjoying the smell and the wind from the ocean, and watching my float dancing to the rhythm of the waves as I imagine some fish circling round the bait, till one bolder than the others launches itself upon it and drags the float downwards.

Most times, before I can react, the fish has already let go of the hook and swum away, the bait in its mouth. So you see, I'll tell him, I'm here but my mind is elsewhere, on a magnificent boat, far away where I can never go. I'm somewhere out on this vast watery expanse, facing the onslaught of the ocean, sure of my ship. The wind is my ally; it carries me and I trust it.

He passes behind my back and I tell myself that this time, for sure, he's going to stop and I'll feel his hand alight on my shoulder. I wait each time, three, four seconds, the time it takes for him to pass me, and nothing happens, I see him appear on my right, in the same posture as before. In a few quick steps he is already distant from me. He hasn't lifted his nose from the ground. He didn't address the slightest word to me, the slightest hello, the slightest sign of recognition. We may not know each other, but all the same we're here together nearly every day!

Perhaps, after all, it's up to me to take the initiative.

He will arrive as he does every day, around that corner. I'll look out for him while pretending to be occupied with my rod and line. He will have the same pace, the same absent-mindedness. I'll calmly rise to my feet. I'll say to him, 'Hello, the weather today is super for walking,' or something like that. 'Oh, the walking is not the main thing,' he'll say to me. 'I come here because there's nowhere else you can be in peace any more. I walk, in silence, I pay no attention to anything or anyone, and very soon I'm somewhere else. At our age, we still have many dreams, and perhaps that's all we have, so you'll understand I don't get bored; my mind wanders as if were a captain on one of those sailing ships of past centuries, when they left their home country for several years, not knowing whether they'd ever return or what they would find in the course of their voyage. Yet nothing could dissuade them from leaving the safe haven of the port. And you, perhaps, when you watch the drifting of your line, do you have dreams of this kind?' The conversation will continue like this for a long time; we won't notice the hours passing. In the days that follow we'll get into the habit of meeting each other at this spot by the sea. He will sit down with me, and everything then will be simple.

Yesterday he again passed behind me without a word, without a sign, without anything. And again I hadn't the courage to turn from my line, my hook, and the unceasing waves that give me solace. But he'll come back again today, and this time it will be different. He'll come to meet me; he'll lift his eyes from the ground and see me. He won't be able to do anything except speak to me. He's going to place his hand on my shoulder and say some word of greeting.

There, he's taking the turning on my left! From there it's little more than a kilometre to where I am; about ten minutes to wait. I have plenty of time to observe him. There's nothing unusual about him today. The same pace, the same absent-mindedness, the same disinterest in what's around him. Now he is ten paces away. Behind me some children are playing; they're making quite a noise; they sound happy. I return my attention to my line, trying to concentrate so the seconds pass more quickly – twenty seconds at most. They pass, nothing happens, he hasn't stopped to speak to me. Now he must be visible on my right. I turn my head in that direction. Nothing there either. Yet he's had three times the time it takes to pass me. He must have stopped to watch the children playing. Maybe he knows the parents and has stopped beside them. Now he'll have to chat with them. Yes, that must be it; that's why he's not yet appeared on my right. This time he either hasn't seen me or has indeed seen me but has no reason to address me. He certainly won't want to disturb me. And if my back is turned to him like this, how can he possibly, without knowing me, touch me on the shoulder and speak to me? It's not possible. It's up to me to make contact, since I have so strong a desire for that. Right, that's what I'm going to have to do. I will do it tomorrow.

My mind at peace, I can now return to my fishing and contemplate the islets opposite, with their beaches of white sand and the yachts riding at anchor — I hear a voice: someone has come to sit down beside me and is asking me, 'Do you see that boat in the distance?'

By the Edge of the Sea – III

'We get lost between the huge tall mangrove roots; our feet sink in the mud. The dead coral, the stones, the oysters clinging to the roots graze our legs; we stumble and skid into the water. We have to leave very early in the morning, maybe two or three o'clock, at least three-and-a-half hours before sunrise, in hopes it will be quiet at low tide and we'll catch a fat bagful or two. Otherwise it will be day too quickly, everyone will start to arrive, the walkers, the runners, those who clean the pavement, and we won't want to stay there with our feet in the water, the cars passing behind us and all the noise getting gradually louder.'

'There are some who use the net, but it's not brilliant here for that; there's too much driftwood floating about, too much mud, and too many small plants that appear from the water at low tide. The best way is still to put down a seine around a clump of mangroves so as to capture the fish during high tide. Two or three hours later, you simply have to gather up those which have been caught in the mesh. In the end it depends why you come. At times it's even better yet by hand with a spear, but you have to be very quick and very skilful.'

'I know some guys who always go on a plate boat, a little wooden one with just a pair of oars; most often there's only two men, and that's best. Or the boat can be aluminium with a small outboard at the stern. Once they've arrived where they think there's some fish, they turn off the motor, or stow the oars, and let the boat drift while they fish with the line. It's fine if there's not too much sea or too much swell, otherwise it's better to dive. One moment you're being tossed by the swell, as you adjust your mask and grip tight your speargun, then you plunge in and disappear under the surface. Once you're down there, everything is peaceful and silent. Nothing but the colours of the sea mingling with the colours of the fish. You look, you wait, and when some nice specimens pass in range of the speargun you just have to be, yes, quick and skilful. Some can stay three whole minutes underwater, freediving, before calmly returning to the surface. With leisurely strokes you then swim to the boat to dump the fish you have tucked under your belt, before immediately diving underwater again.'

'I've seen some who come on foot across the residential areas, a net or fishing rod on their shoulder. These guys won't go further than about fifty metres into the water. They'll go as far as there are still enough big rocks they can stand on. When he's reached one of these, the fisherman gets things set up: he'll spread his net over his shoulder and his folded arm, ready to throw it upon any shoal of fish that passes nearby. With the rope that he's kept in his hand, he'll slowly pull it all back – the net, that is, and the imprisoned fish. Them who use a rod have to be really strong and really tough, as the bamboo can be up to five metres long and have a diameter of at least five centimetres at its widest point. Holding that out from your arms for hours isn't a job for a weakling.'

'Passing by on the road, you sometimes see about fifteen of these line fishermen. Looks a bit weird the way they form a perfect arc of a circle joining the two sides of the bay to the head of the bay. I guess this marks the furthest limit of a small fringing reef, mainly made up of big lumps of dead coral.'

'The women, when they accompany their husbands, always have lots of children with them. These women – unless, unusually, they're alone – don't fish; they stay sitting on the grass, in the shade, and chatter about everything and nothing as the hours go by. They watch their children, the smaller ones, while the bigger kids go to play in the water. They have to keep an eye on the little ones in case they wander near the road, so close, where the cars drive so fast that they wouldn't have time to stop if a child jumped out in from of them. It's especially on Sunday that the women come. The other days, they stay at home and work in the shambas you can see not far from here on the hillside next to two big buildings that have recently been put up.'

'If there's not too much wind they'll light a little fire on the shore. They'll cook a few potatoes under the ash and grill some ears of maize. They'll boil up some water so there'll be hot tea when their husbands come in from fishing just before sunset. All together, they'll head off on foot, tired now and laden with a few bagfuls. If they don't get a move on, it will be dark before they arrive home.'

The five men sitting on the big grey and white rocks piled up in huge heaps at regular intervals along one side of the bay were not exactly engaged in a discussion. They were not arguing and they were not trying, not any longer, to extol their view or their style of fishing. They were just giving voice to what they were thinking or dreaming during their lunch break, in the course of which they had quickly bolted down a sandwich accompanied by a tin of sardines and a bottle of water. Awaiting the hour when they had to resume their work in the heat of the sun, and to give themselves space to digest their food, they had sat down as far as possible from the road, at the water's edge. Here they let their gaze wander and were caught by the magic of this quite sizeable bay, which was enclosed almost completely, in the south, by a string of islands. To the north a line of hills stretched a good four kilometres and then turned east

By the Edge of the Sea

along a succession of beautiful, very popular beaches. Sitting on their rock near the head of this bay, the five men let their imagination go and didn't really notice that what each of them was describing with so much love and knowledge was known equally well to his four companions.

At last they got up, and each of them headed back to his public works digger. In one day they were going to bury no less than ten hectares of mangroves under some four hundred cubic metres of earth from the surrounding hills. They had to pile up the enormous grey and white rocks to form breakwaters that will be effective even when there's a cyclone, thereby creating rectilinear new embankments devoid of any vegetation. Later, once the immense system of artificial embankments and backfill has bedded down and there's no longer any slippage or subsidence, they'll build a three-lane tarmac road, with street lights, which will go round the bay as far as the small stretch of sea that separates this line of hills from the first island to the south.

In three months, these five men will have subjugated a mangrove landscape that till now was still wild, and which will never cease to exist in their imagination, nourishing their dreams and their longing to escape when, on other construction sites, they take their forty-five-minute midday break.

One Tree

When the great cyclone winds come the trees will fall. The tree that fell that night was truly a great and important tree. It was said that its roots coursed underground to the extremities of the island. It was said that its trunk grew so high that it pierced the clouds above the mountaintops and caused the rain to fall when it was needed. I had seen with my own eyes that its branches provided shade across the whole of the village. Perhaps even further, as far as other villages.

I imagine the tree before it swooped crashing down, dragging down with it so many shrubs and smaller trees. To imagine it is to imagine people around it. People come to visit the tree and of course they like to sit at its feet to enjoy a long meal and then a long siesta. There are often children, who climb into the tree's branches for no other reason than to climb and to feel their own strength and daring. Even the bigger kids, the adolescents, have adopted it as their rendezvous. And they are certainly the saddest that the tree has fallen. It was what they all used to dream to be.

A man will never be a tree. But a man may have or not have the energy, the strength, the nobility of a tree. All might have hoped to possess in themselves one day the nobility of the great being that once, in this spot, sheltered their friendships and their romances. Now that the tree has fallen, will not these friendships and romances change, transform, perhaps disappear for ever? It's as if suddenly they had to see life differently, without a guide, without a dream, without an ideal so high, so unattainable, that it would never be limiting. The uprooting of the tree left an enormous wound; left all those who loved it and needed it feeling alone and distraught. They have lost the space beneath it, the games they played there, the tree's shade and towering height, the place of meeting and of memory. They miss the tree as one might miss an elder brother.

No one ever thought, no one imagined, least of all Mireille, that a tree like that could be struck down. When she pressed her back against the trunk and let herself go into a reverie, it would seem to her that it was this tree that held together the island, and not the island that bore the tree and sheltered its endless roots. She would tell herself that the tree had always been there, that it had been there long before the island, long before the rocks and earth of dead coral. Yes, long before this land, long before the extinct volcano, the tree had been there. Its roots had captured the little grains of coral and sediment the currents brought from far away. Little by little a first substrate came into being. The sediments held by the roots hardened to form an underwater terrain that then attracted little polyps. These tiny marine animals have their skeleton on the outside; it's them that build the coral massifs, just under the ocean's surface. Together, the sediments and the countless different kinds of coral that mingle all over them had formed a lovely atoll. It was the tree and its roots that held all of this as one solid and united whole.

Then, under the ceaseless action of the currents and the waves, the atoll was transformed. It became an island of gorgeous dimensions, with mountains, plateaux, rivers, seaside plains, broad valleys debouching in great estuaries into the ocean, and other, narrower valleys enclosed by the mountains. And all of this by grace of the gigantic tree. The tree had enabled the island to exist; it was the centre of the island, in the same way the central pole supported and made habitable the roundhouse in which Mireille lived. When Mireille was resting against the trunk of the tree she had the feeling that she was sitting at the centre of the island. It gave her a certainty of being to sit like that, her back against the bark, so close to the axis of the world. She felt as if she were at the centre of the world, and that made her feel good.

But now the Earth's axis had moved. It had been knocked down – something unspeakable, even unimaginable, that had come without warning, like a thief in the night, its intentions concealed by a friendly face, charming and full of promises. This something had toppled the Earth's axis and Mireille was convinced that the centre of her world, which had been a living being, had now died and that with it everything else was going bit by bit to die or to disappear into the nothingness that would surely expand across the whole country like a dark fog.

This cyclone that had uprooted the tree – not that Mireille would ever wish to refer to it by that name – this cyclone had appeared very suddenly, evading the vigilance of the meteorologists and other forecasters, whether professional or amateur. It had slipped between two anticyclones that, because the cyclone was at low altitude, had hidden it on the aerial photos from the experts' gaze. The experts had announced no untoward weather, except perhaps a few cloud formations at the end of the week. Even these they said would not menace the region for long and, on their maps, these cloud masses of scant importance were far away from the tree. So they had spotted nothing, foreseen nothing, and said nothing of what was really there.

Yet at the end of the afternoon, when the winds change direction, when the breezes swing round, the anticyclones had gone. They had disappeared from both the photos and the sky.

Now you could see 'the thing' swooping down on the island and, as if the tree had been its sole objective, harrying that tree and the surrounding space that lay under the tree's protection. Concealed by the anticyclones, 'the thing', as people later came to call it, had grown stronger, had gathered its forces in preparation for this brutal attack. There was one sudden impact of extreme violence. Then the thing dissolved into the air, as if it had never existed except on the meteorological charts that would always keep a record of its trail. On the island, however, the trace of its passage could never be doubted: the thing had existed; it had accomplished its goal. The tree had crashed down, uprooted for ever, depriving the world, depriving poor Mireille, of its shade and its strength: of its life.

Mireille waited now only for death. Death was surely going to strike everywhere at once, since the world no longer had an axis or a centre. Mireille waited, in despair, could do nothing except wait. How can you live without energy? How could she live now that the very source of her country's coming into being was no more? In the end she went to sleep. It was not true sleep, the kind of sleep that invades you after a long day's work, in which you can forget all your worries and your sorrows, so that afterwards you can focus your energy on one single important task. Her sleep was not very deep, but at last she got some rest and when she awoke, a few hours later, she felt much calmer, less despairing. She was surprised to find herself lying on a mat at the foot of a magnificent tree trunk. She lifted her eyes and recognised the familiar sheltering foliage. She took out the notebook she always had with her and wrote a few lines of verse to which she gave the title 'Before Dawn', for it was a little before dawn, as she remembered, that she had fallen asleep:

> When the great cyclone winds come
> The trees and the roofs fall

One Tree

Wound the Earth
There somewhere under the humus
Life still beats
Drunk on the sun.

Inside

À mon frère

'How could I have left you alone to face the gendarmes?' The man who'd boarded the bus at the same time as me at the Palais du Justice was endlessly repeating these words to himself. Sitting beside him, I could hear them. I heard the heavy, pitiless words beating on the walls of my skull.

But his lips were not moving.

He continued, 'While I was strolling, happy-go-lucky in the streets, strange people seized you and bound your wrists. They took you I don't know where and left you all alone, far away from anyone. Far from me and the others. I could have died from sadness and shame, knowing I abandoned you that terrible day.'

It was as if he were speaking into my ear. I was on the same seat at the back of the bus, a metre and a half away from him, and I could clearly see that his lips weren't moving. The rest of his body was motionless too. He was looking straight ahead, calmly, gazing into the distance as if visualising in advance the journey the bus was making. I saw no tension in his face. The cheekbones were somewhat prominent; the set of the eyes and the mouth, the forehead, everything about his face conveyed absolute calm. The face of a man who's going on a trip and enjoying it, who's enjoying the journey, the things he's seeing,

Inside

the sounds he can hear outside. Yet the strange monologue was beginning to reverberate inside my head. I thought that it should be easy to silence this voice. I turned my head, looked outside, trying to fix my attention on the traffic, on the cars, the people on foot, the shop fronts. For a few seconds I did cease to hear anything. But very quickly the weird voice came back. The man sitting beside me was speaking to me, as if confidentially, and yet his mouth remained obstinately closed.

'When I knew, when they told me you wouldn't be coming back for a few days – three, maybe four – it was like I fell from a cliff. The fall was endless; it felt like it would go on and on, till I lost all sense of time. And all the while I was falling I was in unceasing pain. There must, somewhere, be a merciful power, for at last I landed at the bottom of the cliff. There, I became yet more conscious of your absence, conscious you were imprisoned while I had the whole world at my disposal. You know only too well that I'd already abandoned you before. You know that for months and months I didn't even know whether you were alive. I didn't know where you were and I didn't try to find out. People would speak to me of you and I wouldn't listen, or I would abruptly cut short the story they were telling me. You were no longer in my mind; you were no longer even in my memory. I succeeded completely in forgetting you, in living without you. I succeeded in that until the day you were imprisoned.

'They told me you'd come back in a few days – three, maybe four. A few days of waiting, of doing nothing. A few days of doing nothing and you'll be back. Let these days pass quickly! I'm going to behave differently. You'll have a place in my life again, you'll always be with me, I will see you, I'll come to your house, I'll speak to you, we shall be together. Souls like us shouldn't live separate lives.

'A few days to wait, but nothing is certain. You may know

when someone goes *into* a police station or a gendarmerie, but you never know when they're going to come out. Especially when there's a curfew and martial law. Perhaps you'll never come back. Perhaps you'll never know that you've regained your place in my heart.'

I had some difficulty following what he was saying; his monologue was punctuated by phrases without obvious connection with what preceded them and what came after them. It was hard to disentangle whether he was speaking of more than one situation. Some words, some phrases led me to believe that my neighbour was reliving something. There was indeed a region of the country, very sparsely populated by farmers and fishermen, where martial law had been imposed. Yet it was so far from here, more than fifteen hundred kilometres. A curfew, too, had been imposed throughout this region, but it had been lifted for more than six months and there was no reason now to justify its return; the decision had been taken in panic, and after ten days they'd restored free movement. Nonetheless, it sounded like the man beside me was referring to that period and that distant region. Perhaps he'd just come back from there. Perhaps he'd received a letter from there. Perhaps he knew someone there: a relative, a friend, a brother?

The craziest thing was the way I was hooked on to this voice. I was forgetting the weirdness of that, the impossibility of the situation. How could I hear words that someone was not pronouncing?

It was crazy – I'd stopped asking myself such questions about my own situation as listener. I was feeling more and more concerned about what I was hearing. I was receiving this voice as a real, living voice. The man was speaking to me, I was listening to him, and I was trying to understand him. I was wondering what it was possible for me to do. For a moment, I was on the verge of turning to speak to him. Something held me back. I had the feeling, though, that that instinct was not very strong and that soon I would communicate with him. In what way? I didn't cogitate about the means, about the possible and the impossible. I accepted the situation as it presented itself. I accepted this voice in my head and no longer fought against it. On the contrary, I did my best to keep still. I tried to adopt the same position as him; I tried to maintain the same pose, hands on knees, the same relaxed face, almost serene. I tried to attend to every square centimetre of my face in order to give it the same look as his. I had prominent cheekbones where I imagined I had them; I convinced myself that I had them. I directed my gaze in front of the bus, about thirty metres ahead. And when after a few seconds I thought I had the correct pose, identical to his, I emptied my mind of all thoughts. I hoped in this way to hear better what he was saying to me; I hoped that the phrases, previously incoherent, would link together into a seamless fabric in which there'd be no more holes.

Silence. Not the silence of the voice having stopped, but the silence of deafness. This deafness was already leaving me, I was hearing more, I was distinguishing better the stressed and unstressed beats of his voice. It was like a cardiac rhythm, the beating of the joys and the suffering of a human heart. This voice was a heart in action and I could perceive its every nuance. Little by little, the voice seemed to cease ringing through my brain so loud it might either cause some damage or exhaust itself into silence. It seemed to me that we were connecting in one precise spot in the space that separated us. We were going to meet one another and to find ourselves.

'When you come back, after I've gone to find you. When I've waited for you outside the locked doors. When those doors open, and you've recognised me, I shall take you away. I'll wait as long as necessary, alone or with others, even if the others slope away because too much time has gone by. I'll take you away when you come out and I'll show you the things we always wanted to see when we were children. I will take you to the high mountains of that distant country. We'll stay there a long time, as long as it takes to really feel we are there. We'll go on the long walks you used to talk about. We'll live in caves, we'll eat simply, we'll pray every morning and every night. Short prayers to nature, to life regained. Prayers like I learnt to pray when I fell down that cliff. I shall take you away and we'll discover new people, new ways of being happy, of talking to one another.

'How long these days are! How the minutes drag! How slowly everything goes, so slowly that I fear I'll be an old man when I see you, and won't be able to find the words to tell you what I now understand! Such simple, joyful things. The kinds of things you used to talk to me about before I forgot all about them, before I went my own way, only to come back changed and impossible to understand.

'We'll travel the world at a smooth, nimble pace, unstoppable. We'll put behind us that loss of understanding. We shan't seek solitude, we shan't be hermits, we'll be travellers, mountain walkers. Yes, I will take you away! We'll live together in new houses, learn new dances, new songs. I'll teach you new instruments; I'll listen to the poems that you've written, that I never deigned to learn. When I have you back.

'When I have you back and we can journey together.

'Ah, this waiting is so prolonged, and terrible, and it frightens me. Will it be over in a few days? Do they know what I'm going through? Do they know that each second is like an eternity? No, surely not. They'll think that I am what I seem: a selfish oaf unheeding of your pain, your imprisonment.'

He was suffering but I was not suffering with him. It was not a simple identification. Our lives were our own; our lives remained independent. We were ourselves. I was simply hearing him; I was hearing his heart beating. He was suffering from this other person's absence. He was suffering from the burden of guilt he was carrying. Guilt from this person's imprisonment, guilt from their loneliness. He was conscious they had long been alone. Rightly or wrongly, he blamed himself; I didn't care which it was. I had an urge to tell him he was not alone. He was only different. He was projecting on to the other his own feelings of loneliness and, perhaps, fear. Fear of death. Fear of punishment that ensues from guilt. I did not address him in speech; something told me that it wouldn't be so simple. He was afraid of punishment; had good reason to dread it. Hadn't he been selfish? Hadn't he ignored that person's calls? If only he'd considered that they might love him and be holding out their hand to him? He knew he'd been guilty of pride and intolerance, now that he could see the hand extended, now that he heard a voice speaking to him from far out of reach.

I should say nothing; I should leave him to his waiting and this suffering that would pass.

The other people, the people sitting around us, suspected nothing. They continued their reading and their chatting. The bus had come from the bus station in the south of the city of L—. The passengers knew the route very well – their route – the cathedral you had to pass, the market where you had to wait five minutes, the quay you went along. In the meantime, so long as you'd not yet reached your stop, there was nothing of interest either inside the bus or unfolding outside the windows. An inner bell told them when they were approaching their destination. I saw them, I heard them, but nothing in their faces or gestures stayed in my mind. The bus was always moving forwards. But so slowly. I recognised the particular buildings we were passing, those of the central school and the university. I was surprised we were only passing them now, when so much time had gone by since I'd heard the first words resound inside my brain. I thought of a certain lady. A lady with white hair whom I'd met three or four years before. We had got on well and conversed at length. She was knowledgeable about distant countries, ones permeated with mysterious forces, some benign, others uncontrollable. The more I thought of her, the more her features took form. Her large blue eyes, her unwrinkled face, her hands resting on the table where our cups of coffee sat. Above all, her long white hair. I remembered too her voice, which for a short time now supplanted that of my neighbour, my new friend:

'Strange things are often beautiful if you allow them to be – if you let them flourish. Especially those born from our imagination. Things that seem to have come from nowhere, which you don't understand at all, to begin with. When they come to you, you have to let them live and unfurl, until they express their true form and brilliance. You have to give them room to grow and to ripen within you. You have to love them and accept them when they first appear. They will often be very lovely, if you take them as they are. Eventually they'll speak to you and reveal to you some obscure region of your being.

'I should like to keep you with me longer,' she added, 'but time is pressing, I must be on my way. There are so many places on earth that are regarded as mysterious and are little seen, little thought about, little loved. Perhaps because they're too arid, too empty, too silent. But may they not be silent because often we are too deaf?'

I had loved her voice and I realised that I'd always treasured it, always kept it inside me like a talisman such as women hang inside their bodice and never take off. It's easy to sneer about superstition when such talismans are worn for the sake of faith, or love, or sensitivity, or good health. But they can in certain moments focus the whole of the world, the whole of the universe, and recreate it. How can you understand such a power,

Inside

such a universe, except in faith and joy? Everything is simple, sometimes.

For several seconds, in silence, I beheld the face of this woman who'd returned from my memory. Then the void of silence was filled anew with words.

'I know that you can hear me – that in these circumstances, in this forced solitude, you'll think of me from time to time. I fear your thoughts. I fear what you'll see of me.'

The beating of my neighbour's heart had accelerated to such a point that I feared for him. I was hearing his voice again, overwhelming; it was beating once more at the walls of my skull. In struggling to understand the significance of that, I lost whole phrases. Then silence returned; the connection had gone. I was delighted to realise that. I felt a calmness return to me. Then his voice came back. This time he sounded almost serene, as if he'd come out of the labyrinth, having eluded the fear of dying. His voice no longer banged at me; it floated in the air and I received it without straining. Powerless to fight it any longer.

'You know I can hear you, that I'm coming to see you. I am with you. I'll get you out of there. There will certainly be words that need to be said, explanations to be made. And if I can't see you when I get there, if I can't speak to you, then I shall wait. The things that have happened, the mistakes and misunderstandings, what do they matter now? The distance there may have been between us, the silences and closed doors, what do they matter? We were side by side and we didn't know it. We passed near each other without seeing each other. Who cares what is past? Yes, what does it matter to us? For so long everything weighed upon you; for so long you bore alone your sadness and your grief. Then my turn came; I too have carried that burden. Today it will vanish into thin air. I can see exactly who we are and what unites us. Time can wait. I will be there when the door opens.

'I can imagine, though, the nights you've spent alone. Long and cold and sleepless, haunted by the fears that such places must inspire. I pray that you can hear me and feel my presence. Soon we shall go where as children we used to dream of going. May you know there's no longer any barrier to our meeting. May we understand once again the different languages we speak.'

What dreams were they? In what snow-covered mountainous countries? Were they the countries of which my friend had spoken? The country, perhaps, where you can gather flowers and roots to make teas to relieve the cold and the loneliness, the fear and the immensity?

Imperceptibly that voice returned me to myself. The voice was melting into space, into nowhere. It was disappearing, dying away almost. Soon there'd be no one to hear it. Soon I would no longer be there; I'd be closed back into myself, as it had to be.

I'll try later to remember whether I too, as a child, did not dream of far countries where people live in caves and in the trees. I'll try to remember whether I didn't have someone with whom to dream of such exciting, dangerous journeys – in another life, elsewhere than here where I've always lived and where I feel so stifled, though I won't admit it aloud to those I'm close to, those around me, those I love. Later I'll delve into all that, into my past, my future. For the moment, I just wanted to understand what was happening – for the man was still there, in the same position, looking not quite so much like someone turned into a statue as like a trainee yogi doing his exercises in the bus. I was still there beside him, my posture so close to his, my mind on fire.

To understand! I had to understand! To seek understanding, to find, to imagine, to concoct a hypothesis, to formulate it, verify it, and seek, seek again. I absolutely had to understood what was happening.

Inside

The only explanation I could think of was a sad and feeble one: that I must have been dreaming. Yes, just a dream! A reassuring explanation. I convinced myself that I'd slept badly the night before – which was not the case – that I'd been overexcited, daydreaming to help myself endure a punishing journey in a packed and unusually slow bus. I had dreamt like a child that the man sitting beside me had maintained a fixed position, when I'd only looked at him once. His posture in that one instant must have stayed embedded in my mind. I'd dreamt of a voice, dreamt of questions, dreamt of a curfew, martial law, gendarmes, a man imprisoned. I had dreamt it all. Like a rather sad, lonely child.

Prosaic explanation, isn't it? I had an urge to share this conclusion with him, but then I thought he'd take me for a madman or at least someone rather nervous. So I repeated to myself, 'You've dreamt; you're tired. You're tired; you've dreamt.'

I have not dreamt.

The negation slammed into the midst of my litany.

He was there, sitting next to me; I had looked at him several times, I'd studied his face, I'd slowed my breathing and let the thoughts of the moment fade away. At first I'd felt his voice striking my skull like a physical blow, painful. I'd heard a first phrase from which, I remembered perfectly, all the rest then came: the extraordinary perception of the beating of his heart, the intrusion into his feelings, and in the end the peace and serenity that filled him and would remain in him for long years.

I had not dreamt.

A letter?

Perhaps he'd read a letter out loud. No! I'd seen no paper in his hands. I had not dreamt; something *had* happened. I didn't know what, or how it had happened, but now I felt happy. Later I'll think I've imagined it all; 'always there is beauty in the strange things we imagine'.

By the Edge of the Sea

The bus was arriving at the Palais du Congrès. I stood up. The man sitting beside me didn't get up. I walked along the aisle to the front of the vehicle, feeling the aim of his gaze upon my back. I paid my fare to the driver and descended the two steps to the pavement. I turned round as the bus began to drive off. Just had time to see the man the other side of the window. Sitting alone now on the seat.

He turned his head towards me. He looked at me, then the bus carried him away, leaving nothing but an enigmatic smile hanging in the air.

Alma

It's nearly midnight. I'm waiting.

Some friends were supposed to come for me at half past eleven. 'We may possibly be late,' one of them had said when we parted last night.

They were now nearly half an hour late.

I decided to wait another ten minutes. If they still hadn't come by then, I would make a decision. We had to go to meet a friend who had just arrived back from Cambodia. She had told us she had some important findings to share with us. We – my friends, this girl, and me – were all part of a small society whose central purpose was to research and collect alphabets. You can't imagine how much time and space such an ambition can take up. We had briskly eliminated from our research the ideograms, pictograms, and other phonograms, and even the hieroglyphs, of which there are countless series. We devoted our attention and our passion solely to alphabets in the strict sense, meaning 'any lists of graphic signs that serve to transcribe the sounds of a language', whatever language that may be. And these alone were many!

Think about it: from the first traces of the Cretan Protolinear scripts, almost two thousand years before Christ, up to …

I let my imagination run, picturing in quick succession the reproductions that we had of Phoenician alphabets, which deploy only consonants; and those of Byblos, including a remarkable reproduction of the text engraved on the tomb of King Ahiram, which some date to the thirteenth century before Jesus Christ, although probably he lived three centuries earlier. We also had some parchments, very ancient copies of Hebrew and Aramaic alphabetical lists. Some of these lists included signs used by only one or two tribes at most.

I kept in my own library two of our rarest items. One, a long scroll of the fourteenth century, was a collection of different forms of the letters of Nabataean, a language that after a number of transformations must have led to the Arab alphabet still used today. The other item was a page of manuscript in the hand of St Cyril, who, in the ninth century, began to translate some passages of the New Testament into Old Slavonic, a language that had never till then been written. He had to invent an alphabet, the same one that gave birth to the Cyrillic now widely used throughout Central and Eastern Europe. I carefully looked after these items in my home. We had decided not to centralise our holdings, a fact that gave us cause to meet regularly, sometimes at one person's home, sometimes another's.

The ten minutes had gone by. I decided, therefore, to proceed directly to the rendezvous. On foot it would take me about a quarter of an hour. As soon as I was outside my house, I noticed a wind had risen. I'd not been aware of that while I was sitting indoors.

I had barely taken a few steps before the rain began to fall and the wind to blow stronger. It swept up whirls of dust and the litter of paper strewn on the ground. Without an umbrella, my head hunched in the upturned collar of my overcoat, my gaze fixed more on my feet than on the pavement in front of me, I realised soon enough that I was not on the right road. Upon reaching a junction, I attempted to orientate myself by looking for a street name that I recognised or, failing that, anything else that would put me back on the right road.

Alma

I read, 'rue B—' I had never heard of a street with that name in my quarter of the city. And I was convinced that in five minutes of walking against the wind and the rain I had not had time to come out of this quarter which I thought I knew perfectly. I decided to continue, taking a left this time, for I was pretty sure that I'd taken only one turn, to the right, since I set out. By doing so I hoped to get back to the avenue V— which ran by my house. The weather was getting worse and worse. The rain lashed my face and I couldn't see a thing. There was just enough light from the street lights to distinguish the roadway from the pavement. During all this time – getting on for fifteen minutes by now – no car had passed by. No pedestrian, whom I could have asked the way, had come past me. Of course, at this hour, in this dreadful weather, no one was crazy enough to come out! Not even to visit a friend a few yards from their home. This solitude, added to the chill now invading my body, made me realise that to carry on like this was madness. All the more so now that I was sure I was completely lost – a fact that I couldn't help but find intriguing. Certainly, I didn't know the whole city, or even every corner of my quarter, but, all the same, I surely knew well enough the streets and buildings in walking distance of my house!

So I decided to take shelter under the first porch I came to, or, better, to request temporary sanctuary at the first window where the lights were on. Hardly had I taken this decision than I saw on my right some light that was not from a street light. I headed towards it. The light came from one of the ground-floor windows of a vast mansion separated from the street by a small garden. It struck me that I recognised this place, but that impression did not last. I quickly crossed the green space and knocked on the heavy front door. No one came to open it. I told myself that with the combined noise of the wind and rain they must not have heard me. Lost and chilled, I tried the door, and it opened. They had forgotten to lock it. What amazing luck! I would be able warm up a bit and ask the way in hopes the weather would soon improve.

There was no one in the entrance hall. On the wall opposite the door was a giant canvas where the terrible Yamantaka, upon a background of mountains – the Himalayas no doubt – seemed to challenge the visitor as you entered. I lingered in the hall a moment to study the famous Yamantaka, of whom till now I'd seen only small representations in books. After a few seconds I saw, no longer the multiple faces and bodies of the god, but rather the high mountains intercut by deep valleys from the bottom of which rose layers of white cloud. On these impressive mountains spread immense forests where a thousand shades of green and brown conjured a world into which I was irresistibly drawn. I was aware I was holding my breath, it felt as though I was never going to exhale, and my consciousness and will seemed powerless. Yamantaka had paralysed me, his eyes fixed upon mine as if he were sucking from me a vital energy that would enable him to emerge a living being from the canvas. It lasted long enough for me to have an awful sense of believing I was lost not in a district of my own city but in the depths of an unknown jungle populated by horrible, dangerous monsters. Then, without thinking, I brushed my hand over my face to wipe away some raindrops that were dripping from my hair into my eyes. This simple action had the effect of restoring my breathing to normal. I detached my gaze from that enigmatic canvas and crossed the hall to enter a corridor dimly lit by the light from an open doorway a few steps down on the right.

In the room beyond were a large, heavily built wooden table without any dining chairs around it, a guéridon, and an armchair. On the guéridon, beside a lamp with a shade made of rice paper decorated with geometrical motifs, stood a small statue of Shiva. Shiva in his savage aspect, clutching morbid attributes in each of his many hands. The ambience of the room was not exactly joyous: dim illumination, dark colours, frightening images. That did not make me keen to go in further, but, as things looked no better anywhere else, I took three steps into the room.

There was someone in the armchair.

'Good evening, madam,' I said, without raising my voice too much lest I disconcert her. 'I took the liberty of coming in. The door was not locked.'

An old woman lifted her eyes from her book. She closed the book and calmly placed it on the table. It was an edition, evidently an old one, of *The Golem* by Gustav Meyrink. She looked at me for a few seconds. In much the same way as, outside, the house had struck me as familiar, I thought I vaguely recognised her features.

'O Wilhelm, you have come at last!'

I was speechless.

'I was certain that one of you would remember me and would respond to my invitation. O Wilhelm, I am happy that it's you!'

This was impossible. This old woman could not know me. I looked at her, unable to understand.

'Oh I know, Wilhelm! I am so changed, so aged. But you, you're just the same; you haven't aged, not by a single year. You have to understand: forty years over there, it's a long time. The climate, the food, the solitude, everything was so gruelling. Then there was the anxiety, the terrible anxiety, that preceded each ordeal. I tried to fight it, to stay calm, to breathe deeply; but it did no good. The accumulated suffering aged me by at least another five years. I even believed I would never come back. But, happily, I have come back and you, you are here.'

'But where have you come back from, madam?'

'Surely you must remember! We decided together that it

would be me who would go to Cambodia. But, you see, once I was there I realised how ignorant we were. To bring back a specimen of the alphabet that fifty years after Jesus Christ the adventurer Koudinya brought with him to Cambodia, Koudinya who came from the north Indies and must have seen the birth of one of the Indochinese Peninsula's greatest dynasties – to try to do that, when it was soundly established that only three specimens of such a list survived, was pure folly. Certainly, our contacts were good, but they were connected, all of them, to places of worship, places belonging to initiation lodges, religious societies, more or less secret, of a kind that are numerous in Asia and little known to Westerners. I perceived very quickly that once in contact with them I would not be able to leave them before I had achieved the supreme goal they set us. It took me nearly forty years; almost a year per letter …'

I was no longer listening to her. I closed my eyes. This woman of at least sixty years was not, could not be our friend who'd left us hardly five weeks ago! Alma had turned twenty-five the very day of her departure. We had celebrated her birthday most delightfully, as I remembered very well.

I made myself look at her again. She was continuing to speak to me, but I no longer heard her words. I studied her face. And in her face I saw a number of distinctive traits that there's no denying reminded me of Alma: the hair still very black, which now hung to her shoulders, the slightly jutting cheekbones, a skin that still looked soft and unwrinkled. Only the tiredness of the big dark eyes betrayed an age that could not be Alma's …

'I comprehended that the alphabet is like a wonderful staircase. A divine staircase, in which each letter is a step that you have to master perfectly before passing to the next one and in this way attaining the summit of consciousness – of understanding of a universal tradition several thousand years old. The last two years have been a fabulous time of joy and serenity. Then I decided to come back and find you. Everything this time was very easy. The doors were open. It couldn't have been so easy otherwise, could it, Wilhelm?'

I understood nothing. What doors was she talking about? What ordeals? What initiation lodges? If she were our Alma, she would have spent only a few weeks in Cambodia, just to visit one or two addresses and bring us back an old manuscript. Nothing very difficult! Certainly, life over there might not have been easy, but for a Westerner with a minimum of cash at their disposal it couldn't have been in any way an ordeal! That's how I was now thinking – contemplating the matter as if this person could actually be Alma! Alma aged by forty years in five weeks!

No! This was not her. Surely this had to be her mother. Yes, that was the explanation! Believing myself lost, I'd been driven by chance by the wind and the cold into the home of her mother, who of course, despite her years, retained some resemblance to her daughter. Much as I tried to convince myself of this, I knew it was not the truth. Alma had told us that her mother had died giving birth to her.

'Come closer, dear Wilhelm. I'm going to tell you everything in detail. Everything that happened after I entered the temple, when I'd arrived there after two weeks' hiking through the jungle. Afterwards you can go and explain to the others that we have achieved – you equally, through me – the true goal of our society. You remember that, Wilhelm, don't you?'

I couldn't listen to any more. I stuck my hands over my ears and retreated towards the door, staring at her.

When I felt one of the door jambs against my back, I pivoted round abruptly and fled from the room. I ran out of the corridor, pushed open the front door, crossed the garden, and flung myself into the wind and rain.

But the weather was calming down, both the wind and the

rain, and it had become instead very dark, for the street lights had all gone out. Not a star was shining. I walked quickly, sometimes running. Where a little while ago I had thought I was lost, I now knew my way perfectly and recognised all the streets and buildings, so familiar to me from passing them every day on the way to work. It took me no more than fifteen minutes to be back in front of my house, a little out of breath.

My friends were waiting for me. They'd been getting impatient.

'Hey, Wilhelm, where were you? It's nearly midnight! For a while we thought we'd have to go without you. Let's get a move on. We mustn't keep Alma waiting.'

Desert Dreaming

In the silence of the desert I could hear the thousand noises of the desert. It must have been midnight. The moonless night, the lack of clarity, exaggerated my awareness of the noises and my own breath. I had stopped the car – a pickup truck, the kind of vehicle you can find in any garage in Queensland – at the start of a long straight bit of road whose end I could not make out, even with the car's headlights on full beam. In this part of the country it's not uncommon for tracks like this to run for fifteen kilometres or more without the slightest bend to break the monotony of the drive. Once the vehicle was stopped, I had put out the headlights and was abruptly plunged into the black night that I'd been able to push out of mind while the lights of the car were steadily beaming out before my eyes.

At that very instant, as I became conscious of the immense horizon, I realised that the silence of the desert, previously disturbed only by the noise of the engine that by dint of hearing it all the time I no longer heard, was populated by a throng of noises; noises that revealed life – or 'lives' I should say, for, besides the life of animals, the silence revealed to me the life of minerals, of stones and sand, as well as that of the vegetation, quite sparse, growing around me.

At last I was back in the desert and the silence. All was there, seamless, all naked and noiseless. I sensed at last the thrilling possibility of being a stone, a grain of sand, a faint breath of air. As the old Aboriginal had predicted: 'At the moment when it feels possible that you can become one with the elements in the desert, your legs will give you the feeling they can't carry you any longer. You'll get the feeling of, very gently, going down on your knees while you're still standing up straight. A space that seems to grow without you doing anything will gradually take up the whole space of your belly, like someone has slipped a calf stomach inside you and is blowing air into it – so the calf stomach expands and your belly empties. At this moment you'll know that everything is possible: to be stone, to be sand, to be wind, snake, plant, to be in every part of the desert. You'll know it because little by little you'll cease to have either head or brain.' That's what he had told me; that's what was happening while I was getting out of the car and while I stood there a few steps away from the vehicle, my feet unsteady on the knobbly ground of loose sand and stones, one of which, about as big as a clenched fist, was pushing up my heel, keeping me unstable.

I don't know where exactly in the desert I stopped. Somewhere to the northeast of Alice Springs, which I had left forty-eight hours before. Naked – the word suited the situation exactly: naked the countryside seemed to me, naked the emotional state I was gradually entering as I drove. Tiredness had by then been overcoming me for some hours and I'd had to struggle not to fall asleep at the wheel. I could have stopped long before and slept for a while. But I didn't want to sleep; I'd been awaiting this moment, the moment when you know that you will no longer sleep, perhaps ever, and that this forced wakefulness will lead you to open doors of the spirit that usually are padlocked. Now I had stopped. The naked desert! The silence! The sounds of the silence were going to be the keys, I thought, that would open the locks to give me a thousand visions of reality; reality that I was ever more convinced was only an appearance, an appearance of emptiness and absence. The old Aboriginal had made an effort to describe for me what he saw there where men from outside the desert saw only sand and stones, dryness and heat, and a fierce and hostile sun. He had warned me, though, that it was useless to try to describe this reality; I needed to inhabit it for myself, in my body, through tiredness and sweat, and not merely apprehend it intellectually. But because I insisted, and because he liked me, he told me about his paradise. For truly it was a paradise, he maintained. 'You'll know the moment when the vision is near. Then you only have to stop and stand there, your face to the desert, and wait, without trying to do anything or be anything. You have to forget everything, to forget your body and the place where you are. You have to let the breath run right through you, the languages to penetrate you till you understand them perfectly. You have only to become stone, sand, air, snake, plant – and the vision will be in you.'

So, I had only to be a stone, a common mineral, a simple solid.

I held myself as straight as I could without becoming rigid, my gaze directed a few metres in front of me, seeking to see nothing, to scrutinise nothing, neither the horizon nor the ground. I had only to be breath. Light as air, I was borne away to the foot of an immense rock. The Aborigines say, 'Things exist, all things, life even, all that lives, because they are dreamt.' I therefore dream this rock and I alight there, take root, and extend my arms, my feet, like tiny spines in search of water in suspension in the air. Paradise, I thought, is quite simple to reach. Tiredness and dreaming are enough to give birth to it. It was necessary to be snake; so I snaked between rocks and roots in search of moisture. In this way I passed from one kingdom to another at the lightning speed of dream, from one paradise to another, linking together spaces a thousand paces distant from each other, bringing all these spaces back to the place where I stood, this place where solitude and silence had seized me and pushed me out of the car; to the place where I heard the multiple sound of silence, the place where I saw the immensity of space, like a vision, at my feet; there, standing in space, the earth at my feet revolving to the rhythm of my barely perceptible breath. For a second I closed my eyes. My body filled with music, stone against stone, sand on sand, skin and bark slapping to the rhythm of giant's steps thudding round the dried-out lakes.

There is the dream country. *There* is the country of the man who dreams, and no one has the right to disturb this country, no one has the right to come there without first being stripped naked in the image of silence. *There* is the place of three paradises that are given through the tranquil vision in which they come, in oblivion and unknowing.

That a word may spring forth and many lives be manifest. That their nakedness may pierce through them and they may find among the stones and sand the perfect ground in which to grow.

A noise foreign to the harmony of the desert and the night made me open my eyes. I was still standing up. I had an urge to take off my shoes and feel the direct contact of my bare feet upon the earth. I looked for whatever might have caused that faint noise, the rubbing of skin on something soft. I saw a few steps away from the car a snake easing round a large reddish stone. The tiredness that had left me during the few instants when I stood motionless had returned. The four or five steps I'd just taken had fatigued me as much as a long obstacle course. I could have got back into the car and lain down on the seat for a little while, perhaps gone to sleep. But I could not bring myself to leave this place where the feeling of being immense, the sense of belonging to the desert, was so total. To be a creature of the desert and not a mere passer-by filled me with joy and serenity. How could I allow myself to make any move that would surely take me back to my former condition?

The silence left me, carrying away with it the knowledge that had flooded me in that moment. My tiredness, however, was too great; I lay down there and then upon the ground, on my back, staring at the black space above me. One second, two seconds, then nothing ... night ... sleep.

Someone was speaking into my ear. I was lying on the sand; it was as if someone had lain down perpendicular to me at the level of my ear and was speaking directly to me. The voice was soft, but firm and precise; the words came in a quick rhythm but very distinctly. They penetrated my ear canal with such force that instead of sound it was images that passed through to my brain. The immense territory of the Aborigines was paraded before me. First an uncompromising flat and empty expanse, nothing vertical, an infinite horizon of yellow and reddish hues. There were people in this desert. They were walking in groups of four or five, walking quickly, almost naked, a spear, a piece of wood in their hands, white cloth tied round their temples, white lines and white circles painted on their bodies. They're journeying I don't know where, and I am among them. I pace my steps to theirs, I stoop slightly forwards like they do, I'm moving forwards, crossing the desert, and I sing with them. The song takes the place of the voice. The song gives birth to gigantic rocks, several kilometres long, two or three hundred metres or more high. From these rocks, like an accompaniment, gushes the noise of the wind. This wind is transformed by long flutes – flutes of bone, perched on the sand at the feet of musicians sitting there, eyes closed, as if asleep. Do they hear a voice, do they hear the desert, the thousand noises of the desert, in the silence? Do they give life to these flutes so that they indwell the rocks, like islets in the wide ocean? These rocks are waiting for me; these men are waiting for me, to guide me there. Their songs have created the way, the route. They gave birth to everything that's around me; perhaps they even gave birth to me. The voice that I was hearing once again was saying so many things, was transporting me into so many places amidst this immense land that I was no longer sure of my body. When the voice goes silent, when the song can no longer be heard, I will cease to have an identity in this place and become the inhabitant of the dream. Whose dream? It doesn't really matter. The dream of another man who will in turn be the inhabitant of *my* dream.

It was the rising of the moon that hauled me out of the sleep into which tiredness had plunged me. At this time of the year, the rising moon meant that dawn was not far off. I got up, dusted off my trousers and shirt. A few metres away from me the pickup truck stood waiting, covered with a layer of sand brought by the desert wind that blows steadily throughout the night. When I slammed the car door a thick cloud of dust rose up. The tiny particles of earth stayed suspended in the air for a moment, then fell slowly back to the ground. Thankfully, the vehicle started at the first turn of the key; I wouldn't have liked to be broken down in this inhospitable place, without water or food. I drove for a good quarter of an hour before I reached the end of that straight stretch of road. The track made a long bend round an enormous rock that at this hour was touched with magnificent highlights, some reddish, others closer to yellow ochre. And there, about halfway round the bend, in the middle of the road, a man was crouching. Impossible to get round him, the track was too narrow and, anyway, in the desert, far from anywhere, you don't drive round a man sitting alone in the middle of the road. I stopped. He got up, came to the door on the driver's side. He was an old man, an Aboriginal, exactly like what you see in tourist brochures, and yet it seemed to me that I recognised him. He was somewhat corpulent, flat-nosed, his curly grey hair held by the traditional white headband, his otherwise naked torso garbed with a simple loincloth resembling the bloomers of children in Europe, and his bare feet sure on the ground.

'Can I ride with you?' he asked me.

I signalled yes with a nod of my head. He went round the front of the pickup truck and climbed in to sit beside me.

I drove for ten minutes in a tremendous silence in which neither of us gave the other the slightest attention. I acted as though I was preoccupied with driving the vehicle, although the interminable new straight length of road required only a minimum of attention. As for him, eyes closed, he seemed to be asleep. Suddenly, when I had forgotten about him and was again succumbing to tiredness, I heard him ask me, 'You whites, do you sometimes dream?'

Surprised, I turned my head to look at him. His eyes were in mine and for a few seconds that seemed like an eternity I could not detach my gaze from those brown eyes in which the pupils, blackest of black, were dilated to the extreme. I had the unpleasant sensation that a liquid, more exactly that a tendril of breath was flowing from my eyes to his. It was as though he was drinking my brain and my memory, making his the feelings, thoughts, and images that populated my mind. Finally, he turned his head and I did so too, returning my gaze to the few hundred metres of track scrolling in front of the vehicle.

Perhaps he had perceived in me the images of the night that I'd just spent alone. He smiled and, before going silent again for the long hours of the journey, he said, 'The dream is everywhere; it's in you as much as in me and that's good. 'Cos if you didn't dream, if your sailor ancestors, on their terrific sailing ships, weren't already dreaming, how would they have come here, to this part of the world so far from their home?'

Brisbane on the Beach

Walking at night, when the blackness presses down and there's nothing else you can do, it's so heavy and so deep. David Goodis is my inferno, Nietzsche my light.

Going out one night to shine a light in the dark street upon the truth that I was born from a mistake. The mistake of a man chasing a dream. A dream he'd thought fulfilled before his eyes in the shape of my mother's smile. A smile full of hope but already tired from having waited so long for love to come and open her door. So he came, that man, my future father and hero. That evening, she must have been weary and impatient. The man seemed lovely, and kind, and full of sweet nothings that promised a heart-warming future. That evening, she opened her arms, her heart, her body to this stranger who should have stayed with us all our lives; with my mother and me. Me, a man, a woman, united in love, a beautiful threesome – so often that was repeated to me but now it rings so false. In entering the revelation as you enter a temple, in penetrating the truth like the cunt of a submissive woman, without the slightest instant of doubt, I entered the blackest of tunnels. A tunnel where dozens of detours shimmered with the promise of escape. I went to bed at the end of the night when, hearing the sounds of men starting work in the street, I knew the sun had risen behind the high walls of the buildings, out there in the city. From then onwards, till I'd succeeded in the mission I now had to accomplish, I longed to inhabit an atmosphere like that in which this couple should have lived. A couple so soon parted. I lay under the sheets, the curtains drawn, light and colours banished.

Tomorrow I'll go buy a gun, a magnum, which can sink a bullet fifteen centimetres into a fir trunk. A weapon that, when it comes to human beings, can stop any aggressive impulse at the touch of your little finger.

The woman had been dead some days. Dead from illness. Dead from cold. Sydney isn't a warm city in winter and, without decent heating, anyone with a slight ailment will get pneumonia like you get a headache driving a bulldozer. Illness and the woman had become inseparable, getting up together, working together, going to bed together, like a pair of homosexuals. When one was laughing, the other would remind her of her morbid presence. A pervasive deathly presence that, one night less mild than others, at last achieved its purpose. The pathetic end of a woman so brave and so faithful. I'd lived till these last days with a beautiful story in my heart. I'd stayed alone with the woman because the man had left us so soon. Gone before the birth of any brothers who could have been with me in those years of loneliness and poverty. Gone before the couple could get established in life; before life could be made sweeter and more generous. Before the couple could leave the basement flat too near the sea, too exposed to the wind, the spray, and flurries of rain. Before the man's unremitting work, his twelve hours' absence every day, could pay him back a happy life.

O poor couple, poor family who God in his mercy hadn't wanted to bless or to help! Poor me who'd been lucky to have a valiant and worthy father, but who hadn't known him and had to try and imitate him! I'd accepted everything, obeyed the rule and the word of my mother. During the long years of childhood and adolescence, I'd worked, alone, compelled by duty, trying my best to live up to the ideal my father represented, heroically dead for the sake of his family, his work, and the nation.

That night, in the depth of blackness, hidden from any light, in the silence that encircles all a man's important decisions, I made up my mind. To hell with it all – the dream and the lie, the love of the father, the hero, and of the mother, who's desperate to see in her son the vanished spouse! To hell with all that shit! For I knew now. There wasn't a shred of truth in it. The man was a dishcloth and a bastard. My mother had been a poor woman, driven to irresponsibility and folly. The man had met her and seduced her. He'd shagged her for two or three months, he'd got her pregnant, all the while screwing the whores on Saturday night. He'd gone away a first time only to come back a few weeks after my birth. He'd played the proud dandy throughout the borough; he'd showed me to everyone, flaunted his offspring like a drunkard's puke. And then three months after this return among us, goodbye! Gone without leaving any address, without leaving any money. Nothing ever called him back and certainly not God, as absent from his soul as ever. He'd gone to seduce other poor women elsewhere, to strut about in other pubs, to play the proud dandy for new reasons, forgetting us as quickly as he'd sired his child. Goodbye, look after number one, life's a battle, Sydney a jungle, Australia a vast rugby ground, where after they'd exterminated the blacks they were hunting down the weak. He didn't want to go under, even if that meant he had to let two people go to the wall who were even more ill-equipped to survive.

When his time had come the man hadn't died as he should have. I'd just found that out. I'd also just found out in which city he was living. Not so very far from here, and even had it been the other end of the continent I'd have hunted him there and wasted him!

Why? Because he'd fucked up my life into a such a mess

that it should have destroyed me, and my mother too. But she, she was dead already. He would pay for both of us, one bullet to the right, another to the left, and then I'd leave him to rot in a vacant lot without bothering to conceal his corpse or hide the gun, without even considering any other precautions. Him dead, I'd soon be following. My mind and my soul had been dead since the last word of the revelation, which had cut like the blade of the sacrificial knife upon a chicken's soft throat. Dead as cockroaches crushed by the road roller levelling the wild dirt roads of Queensland. Because of him, and what I'd been led to imagine about him, I will die. I'd built myself a future life, and an image of what I'd be in the future, equally handsome and respectable, hardworking and loyal. The image of what he'd have been after thirty years of graft. Only I'd have become like that in just five years. Everyone would have been proud, starting with that poor woman whose body and soul he'd violated. Because of him and for him, in memory of him, I'd been ready to toe the line, to be everything that society expects of a successful man. Lawyer's three-piece suit, briefcase of a borough official, white shirt and white collar of a pillar of the church, good son then good father, good reservist soldier, good sportsman and bar bouncer; everything. As he would have been, if God had willed it.

I couldn't imagine anything else; I couldn't imagine another life, another future than what I'd worked so hard for in school, college, university, with no compensation of weekends by the pool or a barbecue on Saturday night. I couldn't even accept the idea that anything else was worth attempting. I worked so hard, dragged along by this locomotive to which I'd been coupled since my infancy. But in these last few hours I'd understood that the slightest mistake or failure, even momentary, in the stoking would be enough to make the boiler blow up ... and I'd blown up. During that brief night when everything became clear, I'd realised that little by little I was dying. I'd realised that the last beats of my heart would be those which accompanied the second squeeze on the trigger of the biggest and loudest gun I could find. I couldn't allow myself to wait and put this off till later; not even the time it would take to make a plan or do a recce to be sure I did this right. Any delay might let the lapse of time carry me away from the flame of truth that had burned in me since my discovery that night. And if that were to happen, then I'd be back in what I now knew to be darkness. A life that was organised, guided, scheduled, of which I would never be master; and this for eighty years at least. I had to cherish this flame, to protect it like the cannibal protected his little spark in prehistoric times. I also had to feed it so that it drove me on to the only possible solution, the only fitting way to conclude this supremely wasted life. I knew by instinct that the few hours I had left to live would speedily run by, never mind the needs of my belly. The hours to come and the lead to come would both belong to him. That would be the way to take back what he had deigned to dump in that woman's belly.

Without waiting, guided only by my intuition, without eating or drinking, hardly breathing, I raced at day's end in search of that man. In the lucid spirit that was sure to possess me I would kill him. In vengeance, in hate and disgust, above all in grief. What I'd seen had opened my eyes to the incredible lies of society for which I'd worn out my body and my brain. Knowing that, I could never forget it; neither could I deny it or change it. That knowledge, in turn, was killing me. For years I had completely bought into the false universe I'd constructed. The truth, that single truth, could never leave me. It was like I was sitting on a wall above a precipice: I knew that the wall was an illusion, and this knowledge was logically destroying the wall … dropping me into the abyss. I'd made up my mind; what did my death matter? I had to hide from the light of day; it alone had the power to drag me back into the illusion, and that I didn't want at any price.

Wynyard Station, ten o'clock at night. There are still some people on the platforms, in the pizza joints. The neon lights sputter the best they can their artificial light. I see nothing, neither the people nor the food; I hear the jukeboxes no more than the stationmaster's announcements of departures and arrivals. I know when I'm leaving; I know where I'm going. No need for instructions from an unknowing third party.

Newcastle, half past midnight. Not very far from the station are some not very respectable streets where I've been told I can get what I need. The man is at the rendezvous on the dot. He's a big man, in a hat, terylene trousers, black shoes; not smoking. I approach him in the agreed way. He shows me the gun, I test the weight of it, he shows me a box of a dozen bullets but the magazine's already full so I say no to that, slip him the money, and we part.

A quick walk back to the station – the express to Brisbane goes at a quarter past one, a crumbling train full of dirty, noisy people, who talk loudly and keep switching on the ceiling lights. Thankfully, the noise of this scrapheap of a train drowns out other sounds. I dive into that, concentrating, as if I'm listening to the most sublime music. The noise talks to me like I wanted to be talked to in this moment, when nothing is going to last much longer. Time is abolished; I see beyond normal things. Without prayer, without chatter in my mind, one single thing haunts me, one single action. I know precisely which. I know what will follow and I want it. Perhaps not all of my mind wants it, but the part of me that does is driving me, its momentum amplified by the metallic roar of the wheels on the rails.

When I set foot in the streets of downtown Brisbane the dawn is near; one short hour to go till then. In a few minutes I'll be with him, that foul tramp who lived in porches, who failed in everything, succeeded in nothing, a bum who's going to finish up wasted on a pavement with his head sagging in a gutter of dirty water. As I walked, I wondered how I, in turn, would die. I knew that I could no longer live; the life I'd planned for myself, that impossibility, was now my death. How would it come? How would my body become a corpse? For a few seconds I really considered that question. A lightning flash through my brain – I understood at once. Without any doubt, I would die simply because I wanted to. *I wanted to!* That force will be enough to stop my heart, to block a major artery, to keep the air from entering my lungs. I alone will be the instrument of my death … I went along the beach, the sun not yet up, but way out on the horizon there was already light. It's going to be a lovely day; this will be a beautiful day to die. Very little noise. Silence. Solitude. And then the image comes, brutal, of a dead body – me! – and the pain inseparable from death, while on the beach there's only sweetness and life, the dawning sun and life. Why must I suffer again? Why must I suffer one last time because of this man, at the same time as him, and die?

Little by little the desire to live was stirring. A new impetus was awaking, an energy that I knew was streaming from the sun in this peaceful dawn. Life was insistent. I shouldn't have to die; that was too much to offer him. Nothing demanded such a sacrifice on my part. On the contrary, everything in the last twenty-four hours had been leading me towards another life. With every step this new will got stronger – to live despite everything, to live differently, but to live nevertheless. Like the plants, the flowers, the trees, the wind. Like the sea, like the sun as the days and the nights, the minutes and the years pass quickly by. I wanted that. I will not then die. If I was to have been the sole cause of my death, by my will alone, then I could just as well survive, now the force of my will had reversed, and surely my heart would not stop, the artery would let the blood pass, the lungs would fill with oxygen, and I would live on past the moment the other man died. For that I had not forgotten; the man would be executed as planned, as it had to be. The police? I was happy about them, happy deep inside; nobody knew I was here, and a tramp's death won't pull the attention of the best inspector in the city, so ...

We were face to face. He'd just got up, rudely woken, surprised by the violent kick I'd given him in the kidneys. In a couple of words I explained to him who I was, what I had decided, the sentence I was going to carry out. He didn't even blink, as if he'd been waiting for this all these years since he'd abandoned my mother. Poor woman, poor métisse, unhappy mix of Welsh and Aboriginal. Poor lonely woman, lost in the immense whiteness of Sydney. I was silent, expecting him to make some attempt to get away. Nothing. I took out the gun and fired a first shot. I was going to live happy. But now I realised something. A second bullet was needed. The first had wounded him in the liver; it wasn't enough. Aiming at the heart, I was pulling the trigger. That's when I saw his own hand spring out of his trouser pocket and hurl a knife towards my chest. Years of vagabondage had strengthened that hand and his aim was very accurate – twenty years after abandoning us he was still alive, in this underworld so merciless. The blade plunged smoothly in, at the same speed as my finger, still under control, pulled the trigger.

Sydney by the Sea

Sydney, then, will be my last stop. My last city, my sublime port. Where everything crystallises into one final act, one final fear, one last gesture of love.

The journey began so long ago that I've forgotten some episodes of it. Who was there besides parents, besides friends? I don't remember. But I remember with precision that among all those faces and hands that were smiling and waving neither the face nor the smile that my heart sought was there. I was alone in the midst of a dense, joyful crowd. Alone among some of my family and friends. I was leaving, sad because of that absence, barely responding with the usual gesture of hand or head to those who, warmly no doubt, were wishing me bon voyage. A farewell sometimes oiled with tears. Farewell Norway. Farewell Narvik. Farewell E. It's you that I'm fleeing.

I'd bought passage on the first boat to Liverpool, second class. The best that I could manage. Once at Liverpool, I didn't leave the surroundings of the port. The economic crisis when it came there had found the place charming and had settled in without any promise of leaving soon. So it wasn't easy to find a position on a cargo ship. But I was lucky. Two days after arriving in Liverpool, I embarked on a ship bound for Montevideo as a humble lubber in the hold. One-way southward crossing of the Atlantic, non-stop. 'Between four and six weeks,' the second mate told me. 'Once down there you'll easy find another passage. Us, we're going back to Liverpool.' No, I'm not going back there. From Montevideo I'll head for Auckland, still down in the hold. The depths of the hold were not unpleasant. The heat, the sweat, the men, the grease, the oil, the lack of pretention, the work, and then the sea. Above all, the sea. From down there, in the very bottom of the cargo holds, you hear her from the inside. You hear the slightest noises from the inside as if you lived there, as if she were your home. As if you were in her. Not *upon*, no, *inside*. In her belly, where things move so gently, where the motion is subtle, almost graceful, where things outside cease to matter; where you digest. There the alchemy happens, transforming what a man takes in – food, thoughts, sorrows, fears, and small unnoticed joys – into energy. That energy which alone makes life on the surface possible. For others only. Us lubbers in the hold, we are the sea. We're the sea; in her we're at home. What need then should we have to speak?

As lubbers below decks, inhabiting the ocean, we only rarely saw the surface. To tell the truth, we felt no need to. We had no wish for reflection or revelation. But when at last we did come up to the surface and, for a couple of hours, leaning over the rail of the lowest deck, just above the water, we contemplated the immense expanse of sea, a strange feeling would come over us. It was like contemplating the facade of a house!

Sometimes in these moments I felt as though I was observing from the outside the entrance into a cavern. I would watch the other sailors moving about in this entrance: frolicking, fighting, imagining and thus believing they knew the cavern well. They all believed themselves to be the ocean's lovers. That would trigger in me a mixture of pride and disgust. We alone, us lubbers in the hold, were her lovers; we alone penetrated her. Buried in the depth of her belly we lived to her rhythm. In full communion. Those of us who had these feelings, after a couple of hours or so, we'd look at each other and, without a word, our nausea expressed only in our eyes, we'd gather at the foot of the big derrick. Quickly, in a single movement, as if seized up by the void, we would slide at a crazy speed down the huge, absolutely vertical ladders that took us back to our quarters, three decks and thirty metres below. Back into the darkness, the heat, the sweat, the grease. There we could regain our true identity and return to the sea, guilty and sad at having deserted her in order to become, for a couple of hours, no more than voyeurs.

In Auckland the elder son of the landlady where I found a room for a few days talked to me about Sydney.

'That place, the sea is everywhere. Look, from here, a few yards from the port, you can see her, but that's all. You see her big and horizontal, remote; that's all. Whereas over there, in Sydney, everywhere there, you can see her vertical and alive. You see her moving, like a living thing, sucking into the land everywhere. She fills the slightest bay, the slightest opening. She's bold enough to invade the land right up to the feet of houses that are separated from her by no more than a stair of big stones. At night in Sydney the thousand arms of the sea, the thousand bays are lit up and you can see nothing but her, gleaming black, standing out against the sky.' He talked to me all night long of this city where he'd lived and worked only six months. During those six months he'd managed never to be more than three hundred metres away from the sea. Before at last I went to sleep, I knew that Sydney would be my last port. I was convinced that there I would live as in the womb, as in the holds, embedded in the sea, embedded in her belly. Without the oil and grease, without the fatigue, especially, of the toil in the hold that made us forget even the taste of salt. Sydney will be my place, my city, my home. There I shall live, in the depth of the sea, bathing every moment in her caresses and her love.

A single cargo ship was leaving Auckland for Sydney the

Sydney by the Sea

next day. It was easy to get myself signed aboard; I was ready to do anything on board as the price of passage. One minor inconvenience, this little freighter had to call in first at Nouméa – a small port located nineteen hundred kilometres from Auckland and fifteen hundred kilometres from Sydney – to unload a shipment of logs. We arrived in this port on the third evening just before six o'clock. The unloading which should have started the next day was delayed two days by a dockers' strike. Two days that I spent at the bottom of the hold, going up only to take meals and spend a few minutes in the sun on deck as ship's regulations required. What I could see of the city didn't encourage me to make a visit or take a stroll there, even a brief one. Maybe further away, in the city proper, in the interior of the island surely, it wouldn't have been too bad. But I didn't have time to spend exploring. I went back down the ladders into my cave. We returned to sea five days after arriving in Nouméa. I had to move to a different hold and get set up there because I had the job of keeping watch over the big bales of wool we were transporting to Sydney so they didn't come loose from their fastenings and start swinging from one side of the hold to the other and thereby unbalance the ship. In order to settle in and hang my hammock I had to move several empty crates that – who knows why? – were sitting there. Behind one of them someone – my predecessor in this job no doubt – had left a book. It was dirty and deformed by the humidity but no pages were missing and I could read the title and the author's name: 'B. Traven, *The Death Ship*.' Once my work ended – I had to make a tour of the hold every three hours, which took an hour to an hour and a half, more if I had to redo or reinforce the stowing of some of the bales of wool – I lay down and began to read the book.

And so, over the three days of the crossing, periods of reading succeeded the rounds of cargo inspection and the climbs up to the surface at mealtimes. Never since the departure from Liverpool had I felt more in symbiosis with the vessel's movements. These movements were, I feel sure, the digestive movements of the ocean surrounding me. Never had I felt closer to my real identity; I was no longer entirely a man, since I hardly spoke to men any longer, but above all because I was the water and the current, I was the tides, I was the ocean, I was the sea, the true sea. I was the sea, the inside of her, not her glittering surface.

The book finished, the deep having swallowed up the hero's boat and the hero himself as well as his last friends amidst a terrific storm, I couldn't wait to reach my destination. I knew that in Sydney I would find the wherewithal to live ashore while yet remaining bathed from all sides by a deep, powerful sea. Upon everything I touched, everywhere I lived, she would splash the colours and the softness of her skin. The inside was everything; its darkness and heat had been my universe and my refuge for many weeks, it was true. But, alas, I couldn't live without oxygen. I couldn't continue to live like this at the bottom of the hold. No one, unless he's born there, can stay down there for ever without losing his life. Your strength, your energy gradually leave you, digested by the metal and the stink. Sydney would make me live. We were arriving; I climbed the ladder. It was night. I embraced the city. Sydney.

*

Fourteen years have passed.

The ferry that once again is about to drop me ashore has slowed. Just as we passed under the Sydney Harbour Bridge, that magnificent huge bridge known throughout the world, something fell from it. From where I happened to be, in the stern of the boat, it was impossible to tell what it was. I thought of a big metal girder, elongate in shape, whose rusted rivets had finally given way. I thought also of a block of concrete come loose from the deck that supports the roads and railway tracks. I thought, but later, even now, at the moment I set foot ashore, that it could have been a human being. A man, woman, or child who had accidentally fallen. Although that's unlikely given the size and design of the railings. I tell myself that it could just as well have been a suicide. It's fourteen years, now, that I've lived here, so near you, without having found the way back to your gentle caresses. I went once to see the plains and the mountains, the deserts, the forests, other people, everything, the other cities, beyond Sydney. I came back and turned my back on all that, kept my gaze turned exclusively towards you. The sea is large, the sea is deep, she's there at my feet, and her belly is warm.

From the ferry quay to Sydney Harbour Bridge, it must be an hour on foot, maybe two, if you go along the coast.

Also from Awen Publications:

Exotic Excursions
Anthony Nanson

In these stories Anthony Nanson charts the territory between travel writing and magic realism to confront the exotic and the enigmatic. Here are epiphanies of solitude, twilight and initiation. A lover's true self unveiled by a mountain mist … a memory of the lost land in the western sea … a traveller's surrender to the allure of ancient gods … a quest for primeval beings on the edge of extinction. In transcending the line between the written and the spoken word, between the familiar and the unfamiliar, between the actual and the imagined, these tales send sparks across the gap of desire.

Fiction/Travel ISBN 987-0-9546137-7-8 £7.99

The Fifth Quarter
Richard Selby

The Fifth Quarter is Romney Marsh, as defined by the Revd Richard Harris Barham in *The Ingoldsby Legends*: 'The World, according to the best geographers, is divided into Europe, Asia, Africa, America and Romney Marsh.' It is a place apart, almost another world. Richard Selby's collection of stories and poems explores its ancient and modern landscapes, wonders at its past, and reflects upon its present.

Fiction/Poetry ISBN 978-0-9546137-9-2 £9.99 Spirit of Place Vol. 2

Mysteries
Chrissy Derbyshire

This enchanting and exquisitely crafted collection by Chrissy Derbyshire will whet your appetite for more from this superbly talented wordsmith. Her short stories interlaced with poems depict chimeras, femmes fatales, mountebanks, absinthe addicts, changelings, derelict warlocks, and persons foolhardy enough to stray into the beguiling world of Faerie. Let the sirens' song seduce you into the Underworld…

Fiction/Poetry ISBN 978-1-906900-45-8 £8.99

Lightning Source UK Ltd.
Milton Keynes UK
UKHW041253030620
364356UK00005B/247